MONK

CHRIS PARKER

Print ISBN 978-1-913942-87-8

ALSO BY CHRIS PARKER

This one's for Eddie.

EVERYTHING HAS TO BE SOMEWHERE.
Epiah Khan

PROLOGUE

IN THE BEGINNING...

JERUSALEM 33AD

i THE LICTOR

Despite everything that had been said about him, the man he was about to flog seemed no different from any other. He looked weak and scared. Just as they all did.

So much for stories and superstition.

The Roman lictor's right hand tightened briefly around the wooden handle of the three-tailed whip he had used many times to scourge criminals. He was a master with the whip. As was his companion, standing several paces to his right.

As one, both men relaxed their grip and released the three leather tails. They were all of slightly different lengths, each with two small metal balls attached to the end. The weight of the metal stretched each tail to its fullest. They swung as the lictor positioned himself. He could feel them coming to life. He loved the sensation as much as he loved this moment, the moment before it began.

He rolled his wrist, focusing his grip now on his little finger, feeling the handle secure in his palm. He would feel the scourging as clearly as if his hands were touching the man's flesh. Every contact. Every jump and jolt and rip and tear. Every bellow stretching the rib cage, every gasp as the body sagged.

He exchanged one last glance with his companion. He saw the blood lust in his face. He guessed it was showing on his, too.

'Close to the point of death,' they had been told. 'Don't count the lashes but do remember he has more to face.'

They would remember. They were professionals. They knew how to recognise when enough was enough. Besides, if they got it wrong it would be their lives next. And today wasn't their day to die.

The criminal was tied to a column, bent forward so that the rise and fall of his spine pressed tightly against his glistening skin. He was naked, his lean body stretched, trembling in anticipation.

The lictor rolled his wrist one final time. Then he flexed his rear leg forcefully, twisting his hips towards the target, his right arm following fast, gaining speed as it whipped through the air.

The first lash tore the skin across the criminal's lower neck and shoulder blades. The metal balls hit hard against the bone. The lictor ripped the whip back. Bits of flesh flew up into the air. The first scream came, just as he knew it would.

His companion waited those vital few seconds, giving the waves of pain time to flood both mind and body, before delivering the second blow. He targeted the upper back too, worsening the cuts already made, adding more.

Another scream. Another pause.

The first slight gasp escaped from those in the crowd not used to the realities of what they had demanded.

The lictor twisted his body even more forcefully this time, aiming slightly lower than before. He was smiling even as the lashes bit home.

The criminal screamed again.

The two men fell into a rhythm best suited for their work.

They hit from shoulder blades to calves and back again, always knowing which parts to revisit and which to avoid.

They didn't count the lashes.

By the time they were finished, they were sweating profusely. The criminal was bloody, silent and slumped against the column. Despite that, many in the crowd were still calling for more.

The lictor turned towards them. He saw a boy, perhaps nine years old, pressing himself tightly against a bearded man who had anger in his eyes. The boy was staring at the bloodstained whip, which had bits of skin and flesh clinging to it. He was crying.

The lictor looked at him without blinking. He couldn't remember his own childhood.

ii THE CENTURION

The centurion was thirty-two years old. He had been a soldier for ten years, a centurion for two. He had fought in numerous military campaigns and killed many men up close.

He led by example, always taking a position at the front right of his century's formation, always being the first to reach the enemy. He never let his emotions rule him. He never retreated.

Today the centurion led the crucifixion guard, made up of just himself and three soldiers. Compared to many of his duties it was a simple task with two clear objectives. The first was to carry out the crucifixion. The second was to maintain order.

Today the crowd was behaving like an angry mob. And there were more of them than usual. They filled the narrow street, shouting and spitting, pointing and punching fists into the air. When the criminal stumbled and fell beneath the weight of the heavy wooden crosspiece he was carrying, some men rushed forward aiming kicks at his body and head.

They were driven back abruptly by the soldiers. The centurion made a point of engaging the largest of the attackers. He swiped him hard across the face with the vine staff that was the symbol of his authority. Blood spurted from the wound and the man staggered back, clutching his cheek.

The centurion swung round, glaring at the growing swell of people hemming them in on three sides. He placed his right palm on the handle of his sword. He barked a command. His men made an obvious show of their increased readiness. The crowd pulled back.

The criminal lay on the ground, pinned down by the weight across his shoulders. To the centurion's experienced eyes, he was too weak to carry the heavy wooden beam any further.

The Roman didn't hesitate, pointing his staff at a strong-looking man who had not been involved in the impromptu attack. The man's eyes widened. Those around him tried to distance themselves.

The centurion issued a second command.

His soldiers acted without question. The strong-looking man was pulled forward. The crosspiece was given to him. As he adjusted to the burden, the criminal forced himself to his feet. He reached out slowly with a bloodied hand. The centurion thought he was going to touch his helper's shoulder. He was wrong. The criminal touched the wood instead, resting his palm gently against its splintered surface.

The crowd fell silent.

The criminal inhaled deeply.

He's smelling the wood, the centurion realised, *he's breathing it in!*

'My name is Simon,' the strong-looking man said. He shifted the wooden beam across his shoulders. 'I have this now.'

The criminal smiled. For a second, the lines of pain disappeared from his face. His eyes shone with a mixture of love, understanding and strength. His body straightened, dismissive of its wounds, as authoritative as any Emperor. The centurion saw it and took an involuntary step back. The nearest thing he had ever come to a retreat. He forced himself to hold his ground.

The criminal's smile faded as the anguish returned. The body sagged. His hand fell away from the wood. He turned and looked at the centurion.

The Roman kept his expression as hard as stone and ordered the walk to the place of the skull to continue.

It took less than five minutes. By then the crowd were once again screaming their hatred.

iii THE MERCHANT

He was a merchant in metals. He travelled extensively. As a voting member of the Sanhedrin, the ruling Council, he had political power. Now he hoped he had enough. As he stood, waiting for the response to his request, he fought to keep his fingers and toes from twitching. Finally the ruler of Judaea, the man who was both Procurator and Prefect, spoke.

'You are, you claim, related to this criminal?'

'Yes.'

'You are his great-uncle?'

'Yes.'

'And for that reason you request permission to bury his body?'

'Yes. I wish to avoid my family member's body being placed in a common grave.'

'So your request is based on familial bonds only?'

It was the most significant of all questions, the answer quite literally life-changing.

The merchant had prepared for this. 'My request is based on love,' he said.

'Shouldn't all our requests be based on love for one thing or another?'

'Indeed. I believe all of our decisions should be driven by a love for that which is greater than we are.'

'You are referring to the law?'

'That is one such example.'

'Are you suggesting there are others?'

'I am.' The merchant bowed again.

'How interesting. Do tell us what you believe to be more important than the law.'

'Those things the law is created to protect. I am referring, most especially, to our way of life. Our faith. Our relationship with Rome.'

'A good answer.' The Procurator nodded. 'And you are going to give this criminal your own tomb?'

'Yes.'

'A most generous gesture.'

'I can afford another.'

'Sometimes when a man can afford more than one tomb, he forgets how vulnerable he really is.'

'I am sure that, despite the wealth and power some of us possess, we are all small in the eyes of our gods.'

'How true.' The Procurator shifted in his seat. 'We have talked enough. I will agree to your request for the body. You have my permission to remove the corpse from the place of execution and take it to a location of your choosing for a burial appropriate to your beliefs.'

'I am most grateful.'

'However, you will have no formal protection during this procedure and, given the hatred that was clearly felt for this particular criminal, a show of love for him might well put you at risk.'

'Thank you for your concern.' The merchant ignored the

look of disdain on the Procurator's face. 'I will take my leave now and attend to the matter with due haste.'

'As you must.' The Procurator waved his right hand dismissively.

The merchant bowed a final time and exited the palace. It was already early evening. If he and his fellow-helpers worked throughout the night the body would be ready for burial before sunrise, the start of the Sabbath. First, though, he had to purchase the cloth to clean and cover the face, and the shroud in which the body would be wrapped. He would buy the finest shroud available. He told himself it was the least he could do. The truth of that hurt deeply. No matter what price he paid or how fine the linen, it could not disguise the fact that an innocent man had died. And he, along with so many others, had done nothing to prevent it.

The merchant hurried through the city streets, his stomach tight with guilt and loss, the same damning thought repeating in his mind.

It's just a shroud.

SEPTEMBER, LAST YEAR.
PRAIA DA BATATA, LAGOS, PORTUGAL

i HARRIS

The fat American woman with the dirty blond hair stood up and blocked out the late morning sun.

Harris growled quietly and moved his chair as far to the left as he could. It made no difference. He was temporarily deprived of the star's direct heat. Worse, he could no longer see the pretty little thing wearing only the skimpiest of thongs playing Frisbee in the middle of the beach.

Harris growled again and imagined slamming the four-inch blade of his Cold Steel Ti-Lite folding knife into the fat woman's stomach. He imagined the look on her face as the pain hit and her life began to pour out. He guessed she would die loudly. After all, she was American.

The woman turned to face the sea. She patted her hips and said something to her equally fat companion laying on the sun lounger to her left. Then she strode towards the water, her feet forced apart by her over-sized thighs. She moved, Harris decided, with all the arrogance and misplaced confidence of a person who was proud to have voted for Trump.

The sun reappeared. The pretty little thing had stopped playing and was now lying face down on her towel. Harris moved his shiny, metallic bar chair back to the table and took a sip of his ice-cold Estrella beer.

He came to Lagos every year, always for the last three weeks in September. In recent years he had chosen to stay at the Avenida hotel. It was situated on the main drag with views of the marina and the sea. It had a rooftop infinity pool and a restaurant that wasn't as good as it claimed. The Avenida was the sort of modern, airy place that attracted young lovers wanting to show off their bodies at breakfast, and middle-aged couples who had never quite been able to afford five-star.

It suited Harris perfectly. He was a millionaire who preferred four-star. It meant he was always the richest man in the building.

Harris sat back in his chair and closed his eyes, enjoying the feel of the sun on his face. He stayed like that for several minutes and then he wondered if the pretty little thing had stood up. He was obliged to look. She hadn't.

No matter.

Harris took his i-Phone from his shorts pocket. It had an excellent camera and he aimed it at the pretty little thing, increasing the magnitude until her maroon thong and sun-tanned skin came into focus. He took three pictures. As he considered the best angle for a fourth, a huge, dimpled thigh filled his vision.

'Jesus Christ!'

Harris jerked the phone away from his eye and returned it to his pocket. The fat American woman had returned to her sun lounger. She pulled a bath towel from her bag and began to dry herself. The towel looked like a handkerchief against her body.

Harris checked his Rolex. 11.40am. Another ten minutes and he would need to head back to the Avenida. The meeting was scheduled for 1.15pm and he had to shower, get changed, and then double-check that everything was ready.

He took another sip of his beer.

The fat American woman dropped the towel on her sun lounger and started walking towards the bar, towards him. She kicked sand without noticing onto a four-year old playing by the side of his sleeping mother. Harris saw it as a metaphor for American foreign policy. She lumbered past and went inside. He was right. She was loud.

Harris heard her order two pints of Coca-Cola. He snorted and shook his head. Fucking Americans! No history. No sense of art. No taste.

He pushed his glass into the centre of the table and rose to his feet. Sooner be five minutes ahead of schedule than put up with this contamination any longer.

His mind switched into work mode. Reviewing. Thinking ahead. Considering all possible options.

Today's buyer was new to him. That meant he was new to the buyer. That meant an increased likelihood of a pissing contest until the buyer accepted the natural order of things.

Harris nodded. For all its faults, the Avenida did have an above-average wine cellar. When the deal was done and the buyer long gone, he would enjoy a bottle of Dom Perignon. It was his favourite champagne and the hotel offered several excellent vintages. Harris would drink the most expensive sitting alone at a table in the restaurant, letting all the young lovers and middle-aged failures appreciate his wealth.

Harris turned away from the beach. The fat American woman was behind him, two plastic pint glasses of Coca-Cola in her hands. They were demanding all of her attention. She stepped right into him, her arms jerking upwards, throwing most of the dark liquid into his face and over his shirt.

'Oh, dear God! Why couldn't you look where you were going?' Her voice was worse than the sugary drink.

Harris stepped across and to her left, his hand reaching instinctively for the Ti-Lite. He stopped himself in a heartbeat. It was midday in front of a beach bar and he was surrounded by tourists.

Harris took a measured in-breath and let his eyes reveal his disdain. Then he leant in and whispered in her left ear. The fat American woman paled.

Harris walked away without wiping his face.

ii SANTIAGO

The waitress smiled often and easily. The smile never reached her eyes.

She knew that. She also knew that no one ever noticed. People around her saw only her perfect, shining teeth, her youthful athletic gait and the swing of her long, dark hair. All they ever said was how beautiful and cheerful she was.

The one person who would have recognised the sadness in her eyes was dead. He had died in a motorcycle accident seven months, two weeks and three days ago.

Santiago Almeida. Her true love.

Her *first* love as her mother was increasingly keen to emphasise. That was why she spent as many hours out of the house as possible. Spending more time in the town with her friends. Volunteering for extra shifts at the Avenida. That was why she was at work now. Smiling her false smile. Swinging her beautiful hair.

The man she was serving currently was not a local, nor was he staying at the hotel. She hadn't seen him before. She would have remembered. He was dark-skinned, just over six feet tall, lean and wiry, looking like he could exercise forever. He had close-cropped hair and inquisitive eyes.

She presented him with the simply cooked fresh fish of the day.

He smiled as he thanked her. His teeth were as faultless as hers. She enquired if he needed anything else. He shook his head.

'What is your name?' He asked.

'Ana,' she said.

'Do you enjoy your work here, Ana?'

His voice was strong and soft in equal measure. 'I, er, I like meeting people,' she said.

'Do you enjoy serving them?'

'Mostly.' She nodded, wondering if he was a restaurateur about to offer her a job. 'Are you in this industry?'

'Hospitality, no. Service yes.' He smiled again.

'May I ask what you do?'

'Dog training.'

'Oh.' She frowned. 'You mean people bring you their pets and you teach them how to do as they're told?'

'The people or the dogs?'

'The dogs.' She felt herself blush.

He sat back in his chair, ignoring the food. 'The service we provide is essentially to train protection dogs for people who need far more than just a pet.'

'Isn't that dangerous?'

'No more dangerous than serving in this restaurant.'

'But no one in here bites.'

The man gestured gently towards a middle-aged couple eating steak.

It was her turn to smile. 'I meant they're not likely to bite me.'

'And the dogs only bite on command. The rest of the time they're loving and playful.'

'I don't think I would ever be able to relax if I had a dog like that in the room with me.'

'If it was your dog, not only would you relax, you would trust it completely.'

'But not as much as I could trust another person, surely?'

He shrugged. 'Dogs are far simpler than people. Their needs are less complex, their loyalty more complete. Dogs are too busy living in the moment to be distracted by unnecessary complications and confusions.'

'I'd never considered that.'

'There's no reason why you should have. I'm sure you've got other things to think about.'

She glanced at the fish on his plate. She thought of death. Her eyes watered instantly. She left his table without speaking.

The dark-skinned man watched her walk away and busy herself by the kitchen. He wondered briefly what loss had caused the sadness in her eyes. Then he turned his attention to his meal. As he ate, he focused on his gratitude for the food rather than the imminent meeting.

iii BELLINI

Harris waited for the Avenida's pathetically slow automatic front doors to open and strode inside.

He glanced into the restaurant. There was limited activity. He saw just a few of the usual types and a fit-looking man sitting alone, chewing slowly and appreciatively. He took the stairs up to his room on the second floor.

Locking the door behind him, he checked everything for one final time. Then he showered and changed into a light grey linen two-piece suit, a white shirt and a pair of brown moccasins. He fastened his Ti-Lite into his right trouser pocket, buttoning the jacket to make sure the knife's pocket clip was not on show.

Everything was ready. He had spent more time on preparation than he would on the actual transaction. That was how it should be. Manners didn't make the man, but good planning and preparation kept the man successful and safe. And once you were successful and safe, you could fuck the manners right off.

His phone rang. He recognised the buyer's number. He was still cautious.

'Yes?'

'It's good to drink a Bellini on holiday.'

Harris smiled as he heard the required line, delivered by the buyer's strong yet equally soft voice. It was a voice, Harris had already decided, that belonged to the type of homosexual who liked to workout five or six days a week. 'Room 214.' Harris ended the call. He looked in the mirror. He liked what he saw. He hoped the homosexual didn't try to hit on him.

He heard the footsteps in the hall several seconds before the man knocked on his door. The sound was strong and soft, just like his voice.

Harris opened the door without speaking. He gestured for the man to come inside. He was the fish-eater from downstairs. He was carrying a slim, tan-coloured briefcase in his left hand. He was wearing a dark blue shirt with a button-down collar, tight-fitting blue denim jeans and a pair of Nike trainers.

Harris closed the door and locked it fully. He made no attempt to follow the buyer into the room. Instead he remained where he was and said, 'I have the object so if you have the agreed amount this matter will be concluded very quickly.'

'The payment is here.' The buyer raised the briefcase slightly. 'First, though it's necessary to ensure that the object is genuine.'

'You'll get to see it when I've counted the money.'

The buyer smiled. 'No. Sellers always show their wares first. That's how they create buyers.'

'You've seen the photos. That's proof enough at this stage.'

'No.' The buyer smiled again. 'You provide the object for examination. If it is genuine you can count the money. Once you are satisfied, the transaction can take place.'

Harris frowned. 'That's not how I do business.'

'Then, sir, we are not going to be doing business today.'

'That's just fucking ridiculous!' Harris raised his voice.

'You've come here because I have something you want, and you'll fucking lose it if you treat me like a run-of-the-mill street trader!'

'You are most definitely not run-of-the-mill, sir. And how we proceed is up to you entirely.'

'You're not the only person keen to purchase this object,' Harris said angrily. 'I can make a phone call the minute I kick you out. So – and this is your last chance – show me the money or fuck off.'

The buyer blinked. Harris knew that he had won. 'Finally we understand each other,' Harris said. 'I knew we would.'

The man placed the case on the large double bed and opened it.

The sight of the money drew Harris forwards. He sat on the white duvet, put the case on his lap and began counting. He took his time, enjoying the feel of the crisp, fresh notes.

'It's all there,' he said finally.

'Of course.'

'My turn.' Harris stood up. Reaching under the duvet he produced a cardboard picture box. He opened it and removed a painting protected by two layers of wrapping.

'Here.' Harris offered the painting. 'Giovanni Bellini's

Madonna with Child, tempera on panel, painted approximately 1430 AD.'

The buyer took it carefully, reverentially, in both hands.

Harris saw him assessing the validity of the work. He could almost hear the man's thoughts as he checked each aspect.

The dark night in the top left-hand corner.

The less-dark cloud above the Madonna's head.

The lighter, possibly sunlit, clouds above and beyond her left shoulder.

Her eyes fixed on the child.

His surprising reddish, curly hair. His full, rosy cheeks.

The maroon, dark-blood colour of her gown. The burn marks around the edges of the panel.

With his inspection complete the buyer said, 'The accepted truth about this painting is that it was destroyed in a Berlin-Friedrichschein flak tower in an area under Russian control in the early 1940s.'

'Now you know that isn't true.'

'Yes.' The buyer kept his gaze on the Madonna. 'So many truths,' he murmured. 'So many lies.'

'We're not here to discuss philosophy,' Harris said. 'But you can take this as a parting gift: the greatest truth is money. Now, pack your painting and take it to wherever or whomever it's going. I have a date with a sixteen-year-old.'

The buyer raised an eyebrow.

'It's a bottle of champagne. Sadly.' Harris smirked. 'In my experience, it will go down more easily than most sixteen year olds.'

The buyer placed the painting very deliberately on the white duvet. 'Mr Harris, the truth is that for over fifteen years you have earned great sums of money selling a range of religious artefacts and artwork stolen at one time or another from the Holy Mother

Church. These are objects of great importance, many of them are of great spiritual value.'

'I'm not a thief.' Harris said.

'Of course not. This is where you belong, at the end of the chain, taking minimal risks, convincing yourself of your importance and power.' The buyer's eyes narrowed. 'Please, tell me the names of the individuals you work for.' Harris stepped back a pace and reached into his trouser pocket. The Ti-Lite came free and opened with a reassuring click. He pointed it at the other man's throat. 'You really should have fucked off with your picture!' He snarled. 'Because now I'm going to keep it and your money!'

'Please,' the buyer said again. 'Say the names.'

'No fucking chance!' Harris inched forwards, circling the knife, keeping the point fixed on its target.

'Please.'

'I've always wanted to stab a gay fucker!' Harris raised his left hand suddenly, pointing high over the buyer's right shoulder. 'Look!'

It was his favourite trick. His previous victims had found it impossible to resist the urgent visual cue. As they turned their heads Harris had lunged forwards, opening their throats with a powerful slash from left to right.

Now his knife hand flashed forwards, faster than his words. He was irreversibly committed to the action before he realised things were not going according to plan. The buyer had ignored the distraction. Not only that he was moving low, inside the arc of Harris's attack.

The buyer's right hand came upwards, punching into Harris's chest, ending his forward momentum. It was only as the buyer withdrew his arm that Harris saw the curved, six-inch blade in his hand. The buyer sprang back. Harris heard the air rushing out of his own mouth. He realised he had dropped his knife and saw the blood soaking his shirt. He fell to his knees. His last realisation was that the other man had given him room to collapse and die. His last breath tried to carry some words but failed.

The darkness hit him like a train.

The buyer took a white handkerchief from his pocket and cleaned the blade calmly and methodically. Then he returned it to the sheath inside the right pocket that had been adapted for hidden carry. He went into the bathroom and washed his hands thoroughly before returning the painting to the cardboard picture box. He put it and the money into his briefcase. He left that on the bed whilst he checked the room for hidden cameras.

Then he stood beside the body, brought his hands together in front of his chest and said a quiet prayer.

THE PRESENT DAY

PART I

THE MAN KNOWN AS...

1

The man known as Raphael Ward shouted angrily and took a threatening step forwards, raising his right fist as he did so. The young, blond-haired woman held her ground. 'I'm gonna kill ya!' Raphael snarled as he took another step.

The woman didn't flinch.

Raphael lunged forwards. The German Shepherd dog met his rush head on. The woman encouraged him, giving the dog the full length of the black, leather lead. She was pulled forwards as the Shepherd strained to attack.

Raphael pulled back half-a-step, just out of reach of the bared teeth. He stamped his leading foot into the ground, shouting as he did so. The Shepherd reared up, barking furiously. The woman leant back, using all of her strength and weight as a counterbalance to the dog's forward momentum.

Raphael stamped a second time and then stepped forwards, throwing a punch. The dog's bark turned into a bite, latching on to his forearm as Raphael's arm swung through the air. He was prepared for both the impact and the pressure. He provided the necessary resistance until the blond woman ordered the dog to release. It did so immediately, maintaining its place between Raphael and her, panting with excitement, ready to attack again.

'Good boy!' The woman offered encouragement. The Shepherd barked again at Raphael who backed away, bringing the exercise to an end.

'Falco, heel.' The woman spoke calmly. The dog turned a tight circle and positioned itself next to her left ankle. 'Sit'. The dog sat and looked up at its handler. 'Good boy,' she said again. The dog's tail wagged. 'He's willing, isn't he?' The woman looked at Raphael.

'Willing', the dark-skinned, wiry man agreed. 'But he's still not one hundred per cent committed. He's still holding back on the bite.'

'Bless the beautiful Falco,' the woman scratched the top of the Shepherd's head. The tail wagged furiously. 'He's a big, strong boy who's just too kind for this type of work.'

'That's certainly how it's looking.' Raphael flexed the fingers of his right hand as he removed the protection jacket. He was wearing a black Nike tracksuit and running shoes. 'He can still be felt. He's just not giving it everything he's got. Despite everything we've tried, we've failed so far to turn this into his favourite game.'

'And it needs to be.'

'Gemma, you know that as well as anyone. In the hierarchy of what dogs value, biting should be at the very top. That's why we never reward them when they bite. The act should be reward enough. Falco, though, prefers to have his ears rubbed.'

'He is still only a youngster.'

'He's twelve months. He's not a baby anymore.' Raphael gestured to the kennels that lined two sides of the quadrangle they were standing in. 'We've got several dogs that are his age who are already far keener.'

'Dogs learn at different speeds, just like people.' Gemma said. 'And you don't have to be a baby to enjoy being fussed.'

'True. But if your purpose is protection, you should enjoy doing that more than anything else.'

'Not every dog makes the grade, irrespective of their breed,' Gemma countered. Some are just too edgy – too naturally hyper – and some are just too instinctively laid back. Falco falls into the laid back and empathetic category.'

'Then maybe he should go somewhere else and be trained as a therapy dog?'

'Maybe he should come home and live with me as a perfectly normal pet?'

'You've taken your time getting around to that.' Raphael smiled.

'What do you mean?' Gemma blushed.

'You've had a soft spot for Falco ever since you first laid eyes on him.'

Gemma's blush deepened. 'When are you going to make your final decision about him?'

'Soon.'

Raphael watched the young woman struggle to contain the next, obvious question. She was twenty-three years old. He had known her for seven years, since the day she had appeared unbidden at his Derbyshire kennels asking for part-time work.

She had a dream, she said, of becoming a trainer of protection dogs. She wanted to have her own business. She wanted to know everything about the different breeds of dog he trained – German Shepherds, Belgian Malinois, Dutch Herders and the occasional Doberman Pinscher. And she wanted to know everything about him.

He had been intrigued and impressed. Intrigued by her motivation. Impressed by her self-confidence and desire. It had been an easy and immediate decision. 'If you're willing to start at the very beginning and do exactly as you are told, you will learn everything you need to know,' he had said. 'And you will get paid the going rate into the bargain.'

She was so excited by his offer she missed the fact that he had not promised anything about himself.

Now, nearly seven years later, he loved her as a daughter. At least, how he imagined fathers loved their daughters. Now, whenever he went away on one of his frequent trips, Gemma ran the kennels for him.

And she did it brilliantly.

His clientele ranged from global business leaders to world famous sportsmen and women, celebrity figures and royalty. No one complained when he was away. In fact, a Saudi prince had even offered to fund the start-up of Gemma's own kennels. She had refused, claiming she still had much to learn.

Raphael had watched the fear dance inside her. It was the fear of acknowledging just who you were and what you were capable of. He had promised himself that he would train her to deal with it, teach her how to turn it into her favourite game. And he could do that. It was, after all, the nature of his business.

Train. Build a relationship. Train some more. Release.

Begin again.

It was a cycle of behaviour he had mastered.

'So, when is soon?' Gemma's voice cut through his reverie.

'What?'

'When is soon? When will you decide what to do with Falco?'

Raphael looked at the young woman then at the dog, then back into Gemma's sea-blue eyes. 'In another couple of months,' he said. 'Maybe a little bit longer.'

'And then?'

'Then Miss Gemma Morris you will be the first person to

learn of Falco's future. You won't, however, be asked for your approval or your permission.'

Her eyes squinted. 'Every time you try to go all business-like and corporate with me, I know you are bluffing. I know it means you have plans that you're not sharing.'

He bit back a smile. 'Is that so?'

'It certainly is. I know you far too well Mr Raphael Ward. In fact, I probably know you better than anyone else on this entire planet,' she considered briefly, 'with the possible exception of Mia, of course. And, to be fair, she doesn't really count.'

'Because?'

'She's a dog! And dogs don't know people in the way that people know people.'

'That's true. They know people in different ways.'

'That's right.' Gemma paused, waiting for him to continue. He didn't. 'So...?'

'So now it's time for Mia's run up there,' he gestured to the nearby hills, 'And, as ever, you will be in charge whilst we're gone. OK?'

'I was born to be in charge.' Gemma grinned.

'You'll get no argument from me about that. And the day you actually realise the truth of it, is the day you'll be ready to leave.' Raphael turned and walked away.

Gemma felt the fear swirl in her stomach as she thought once again about creating her own business. She put her hand on Falco's head for comfort.

2

Mia was waiting expectantly. She was sitting by the gate in her personal run at the back of his house. Her brown eyes were fixed in his direction. Her ears were pricked, her mouth open. Her brindle fur shining in the Autumn sun. She stood when she saw him.

Raphael smiled when he saw her. She was his dog, a Dutch Herder, four years old and twenty-three kilos of muscle. She was the perfect companion for a man who had no human friends, who had chosen instead to base his life on secrets and solitude.

Raphael had bought her from a specialist breeder in Holland. He had trained her personally. Now she was as capable as any protection dog could be. She was accepting of people and other animals, confident in all environments and on all surfaces, untroubled by sudden noises or movement. She was alert to the earliest signs of threat and able to shift into attack mode in a heartbeat. She was utterly fearless. She expected to win. Raphael had trained her to. He had also trained her to attack with different levels of severity according to the command he gave.

That wasn't a service he offered to his clients. The dogs he sold were all able to threaten or attack. None of them, however, were trained to kill. Mia was. Raphael had kept that part of Mia's training away from everyone, especially Gemma. He didn't want her to ask questions he wouldn't answer. He certainly didn't want her to doubt how well she knew him.

Raphael opened the gate to Mia's run and stepped inside. She automatically sat again, her eyes never leaving him. He touched the top of her head with his fingertips.

'Come.'

He turned out of the run without looking back at her.

She was at his left heel instantly.

They walked across the quadrangle at an ever-increasing pace. They both looked ahead, ignoring the noise and movement around them as Gemma and the part-time staff went about their daily work.

Raphael shifted his focus, emphasising the feel of the planet beneath his feet, relaxing his body in preparation for the forthcoming run, controlling his breathing. Mia matched him effortlessly.

The pair passed through the open wooden gates with discreet bronze signs, reading *Sanctuary Dogs*, attached to the stone pillars on either side. They turned right along a narrow pathway and right again fifty metres later into an open, grassed field. Raphael also owned this. It was where much of the dog training took place.

He broke into a steady jog, clicking the middle finger and thumb of his left hand and pointing ahead with his forefinger. Mia raced on, grateful for the release. Within a couple of minutes Raphael had crossed the field and was climbing over the stile that marked the start of the winding route to the top of the hills. They provided a powerful, sometime stark, backdrop to his property. They were also the perfect place to exercise.

Nature's gymnasium, he told himself as he felt the gentle

beginnings of the slope. He picked up his pace. Mia knew the route. She was always ahead, letting her nose draw her this way and that, whilst checking every thirty seconds or so on his position.

The run to the summit took forty minutes. Neither man nor dog was breathing heavily when they arrived. Mia continued her nose-down exploration. Raphael took his mobile phone from his pockets and placed it on a rock. Then he stood still, facing the horizon, his feet shoulder width apart.

He closed his eyes and shifted his awareness into the back of his brain and body. When it felt as if his consciousness had transferred into the occipital lobe and cerebellum, near the back of his skull, he moved his focus to the base of his spine and from there down the rear of his legs to his feet. His toes flexed automatically, gripping the soles of his shoes, seeking connection with the Earth.

Raphael focused on the feeling for a few, joyous seconds and then returned his attention to the base of his spine. He let his torso stretch gently upwards. Then he imagined his fingers reaching down towards the Earth. His hands moved instinctively in front of his thighs. Raphael closed his eyes.

He had stopped thinking from the moment he had begun the exercise. Now he inhaled gently through his nose. He felt the air circulating inside his body. He felt his heart beating. Then he exhaled slowly through pursed lips. As he did so, his relationship with his body changed. He could feel it around him, but it was distinct from whom he really was. Rather it felt like a covering, some strange sort of mix between clothing and a car.

Raphael opened his eyes.

Opening the curtains, as Pietro, his first teacher, had called it. It was a practice in seeing. Not in the way the vast majority of people saw things, blinkered by their beliefs and expectations.

This was seeing things as they truly were. Pietro taught that it was a skill dependent upon forgetfulness. The way to remove prejudice was to forget everything you thought you already knew, to see someone or something as if for the first time.

Whenever Raphael stood on the summit, he began his training routine with this activity. Feeling his connection between the Heavens and the Earth, forgetting the view he had seen a thousand times.

Today it was filled with Autumn colours. Raphael was rocked by the vibrancy of the season as it flooded his vision. He staggered back a pace. Mia was suddenly by his side. He kept his gaze fixed.

'It's alright, girl,' he said. 'Everything's good.' Mia lay down.

Raphael focused on his breathing for several minutes, letting his eyes absorb the shapes, movements and relationships of the landscape. Then he turned his back on it all and committed himself to the second part of his routine.

Yoga.

He began with a sun salutation before moving on to a series of warrior poses. The energy inside him grew as he worked his way through the ancient postures. He ended with a headstand, feeling the increased blood flow to his brain and the release in his spine.

When he came back to his feet, Raphael took three deep breaths and reached inside his tracksuit top. The knife was snug inside its shoulder sheath. It came free easily.

The curved six-inch blade glinted in the sun.

3

Mia watched him expectantly. Raphael ignored her and began to move, turning in tight circles over the uneven ground. His footwork was light and assured. The knife flashed in front of him, thrusting and slashing, weaving figure of eight patterns through the air. Occasionally he dropped low. Sometimes he rolled, coming back to his feet with the knife blur fast as he countered and then attacked his imaginary opponents.

During one roll he changed his grip on the weapon. Now the blade ran along the inside of his forearm, hidden from view until he extended it in a series of interconnected thrusts and slashes.

After fifteen minutes he changed the knife from his right hand to his left; a move so swift it was barely perceptible. Sweat beaded his face. The training continued. Towards the end Raphael began combining empty hand blows, elbow strikes and low-line kicks with the knife attacks.

Mia quivered with anticipation. She knew her time was near.

One final flurry, a sudden change of height, and when Raphael straightened the knife had been returned to its sheath.

Mia barked once and launched her assault. Raphael spun to

face her, his right arm rising across his chest as she leapt towards him, teeth bared. In the last instant, just as her teeth were about to bite down on his flesh, Raphael pivoted away to his left. Mia instinctively twisted her head to follow him, but her momentum was too great and she flew past.

It took less than a second for her to regain her footing. This time she came at him low, snapping at his Achilles and hamstrings, fury in her eyes. Raphael danced away, taking the opportunity to unbalance her by pushing the sole of one foot against her shoulders whenever he managed to move outside her line of attack.

Without warning Mia changed again, feinting low then snapping up towards his groin. He used his left shin against the side her neck, a well-timed thrust strong enough to knock her over without damaging her. She growled as she returned to the fray.

Raphael grinned. This was a training session for her as much as it was for him. He loved watching her intelligence at work, the way she learnt and adapted in response to his counters, the way her confidence never wavered. He loved the connection he felt with her.

Mia moved to her right, sinking down before suddenly leaping high aiming for his throat. Raphael dropped to the ground, reaching up with his right hand as he fell, catching her in her stomach, tipping her head over heels in mid-air. He landed in something close to a full side-split but was back on his feet almost instantly. So was Mia.

Raphael sank into a low stance and offered his left arm as a target. He saw her consider it briefly. His grin widened. She hurtled towards him. He prepared to move.

His mobile phone began to ring. 'Enough!' Raphael raised his hand. Mia stopped abruptly.

'Down.'

Mia lay.

'Good girl.' Raphael strode over to the rock and picked up the phone. He recognised the number.

'Yes?'

'I have something for you.' It was, indeed, the well-known voice.

'I am happy to receive it.'

'I wouldn't expect anything less. Only this time I need to discuss it with you in person. This time we need to meet.'

Raphael's heartbeat quickened. 'That has never been necessary before.'

'No.'

The voice fell silent. Raphael knew better than to wait. 'I will travel to wherever you require,' he said.

'You will not have far to go.'

'I don't understand.'

'There is a most unusual urgency. So I am already nearby. I will see you at 2pm. You will be informed where.'

The phone went dead.

Raphael ran his left hand over his close-cropped hair.

Not just a meeting, but also a visit.

A most unusual urgency.

What on God's good Earth could be of such importance that all protocol was broken? Questions began to swirl inside Raphael's mind. Desperate to clear them, he closed his eyes and turned in the direction of the horizon. He tried to feel the ground beneath his feet. He tried to let his spine stretch up towards the sky. He couldn't do either. His mind filled with an image of the landscape. He couldn't lose it. He finally accepted defeat and opened his eyes.

Mia watched from a distance.

4

The run back to the kennels took less than thirty minutes. Raphael fed and watered Mia and went inside. His house was a three-bedroomed detached property built on the western side of the compound. The front faced out onto the quadrangle. The rooms were all furnished simply. They were all spotlessly clean.

Raphael went upstairs. He undressed in his bedroom and showered in the white tiled bathroom on the other side of the landing. He took a cold shower. He always did. His body didn't flinch when the water hit his skin. He took his time, hoping the cleansing would help clear his mind.

It didn't.

Raphael dried his body vigorously and put on a clean black tracksuit. He walked barefoot downstairs and opened a door in the stairwell. A series of unlit steps led down into the basement. Raphael moved onto the first and closed the door behind him. It was heavy and soundproofed. Raphael welcomed both the darkness and the silence as he walked down the steps slowly and confidently.

The basement floor was cold beneath his bare feet. He took three paces to his right, to where he knew the square black cushion was positioned. He sat on it, assuming the lotus position, resting his hands together in his lap, the left on top of the right. He closed his eyes. The meditative state dissolved his senses.

Raphael had been drawn to meditation even before Pietro had begun teaching him. As a boy he would often slip out of the house late at night to sit, meditating and praying, at the foot of the aged stone pine tree that dominated their garden. He kept this a secret from everyone apart from Father Antonio, the local Catholic priest. 'The Lord is calling you,' the old man had said. 'Keep listening, keep following his call.'

Raphael had. His study of the Gospels had been followed by the study of lesser-known Christian texts. He spent hours of every day in meditation and prayer. Father Antonio began referring to him lovingly as the town's mystic. Eventually, even his parents accepted their son's unusual life path. It was a path that changed forever when Father Antonio introduced him to Pietro.

Now, as Raphael sank deeper into his meditation, he felt the internal space drawing him in. For years it had been a source of strength and comfort, emptiness as vast as the Universe and, in the same way, home to everything. Only of late, the emptiness was being disrupted by ever-increasing feelings of uncertainty and doubt and an occasional strange, fleeting image of what seemed to be a road.

Today the feelings hit suddenly, tugging at his gut. Raphael sought retreat in the space and the darkness.

A blurred image of the road appeared in front of him, stretching into the distance. Some part of him wanted to step onto it, but the road disappeared before he could. The darkness threatened to dissolve. Raphael forced himself to continue his practice.

Above him, at ground level, Gemma and the team continued their work in the brightness of the Autumn morning.

5

The Cavendish Hotel looked at its best in this season. Dean Jones had come to realise that during his first year as hotel manager. Something about Autumn colours enhanced the sun-scrubbed sandstone of the building and the beauty of the grounds and parkland beyond. No surprise then that the hotel's rooms were filled with couples seeking a romantic get-away.

The latest arrival, though, was alone. He was clearly here for a business meeting. Dean guessed it would last no more than an hour and that purchases would be limited to a coffee or two. Still, every guest deserved the best possible service. So, Dean smiled and led the bald, over-weight, well-dressed man into the comfortable bar. It was empty, as it usually was mid-afternoon when the weather was good.

'Where would you like to sit, sir?' Dean gestured vaguely around the room.

'This is fine.' The man chose a corner table and sat without being invited further.

'Excellent.' Dean smiled again. 'Can I get you a drink and some food perhaps?'

'A coffee. Americano. Black, no sugar.'

'Of course.' Dean turned abruptly and went to work behind the bar. He hadn't finished making the coffee before a second man joined the other. It was clear to Dean that this was not a meeting of equals. The newcomer was obviously subservient in his manner. In fact, although his back was to the bar, it looked as if he actually kissed the bald man's hand as he greeted him.

Dean returned with the drink. 'One Americano, sir. And for yourself?' He looked at the newcomer.

'Just water, please.' The voice was soft, yet with more strength than Dean had expected.

'Certainly.'

Neither of the men spoke until Dean had poured a small bottle of mineral water and left the bar.

'So,' the bald man said, 'here we are. Finally.'

'Yes.'

'There is no one more experienced at managing our specialist operatives than me.' The bald man looked up at the ceiling as he spoke. 'And there is no operative with more experience than you.'

'Thank you.' Raphael inclined his head.

'You have made my life easy where others have not. Once you are unleashed you can be relied upon to track down the target and return home with the desired object. Have you, I wonder, kept count of the many precious things returned by your own hands?'

'No.'

The bald man brought his gaze away from the ceiling and stared at Raphael. 'It is a rare hunter who does not keep a record of his successes.'

'It is an arrogant servant who records how many times he pleases his Master.'

'Very good.' The bald man's smile was tight-lipped. He crossed one leg over the other; his raised left foot jabbing in the air as he talked. 'It has been my practice to meet operatives only if they have created a problem of significance. That is why we have never met.'

'And now?'

'Now I am here to impress upon you the absolute importance and urgency of the task you are about to undertake.'

Raphael straightened in his chair. That word again. *Urgency*. And never before had he heard this man use the phrase *absolute importance*. There were few things that could warrant a change in his approach and only one that could be referred to as *absolute*.

Raphael raised his level of awareness, looking over the other man's shoulders, letting his peripheral vision dominate. Opening the curtains.

He saw the pallor of his handler's skin, due no doubt to spending most of his time indoors. He saw flecks of alcohol-induced violet in his cheeks, the lack of emotion in his eyes. He saw the cut and quality of his grey, pin-striped suit, how it contained and disguised his overweight body. He saw the shine of his fine Italian shoes and the un-scuffed sheen of the raised leather sole.

Those shoes have never walked the streets.

The realisation flitted through Raphael's mind. He let it go. The bald man was about to speak again.

'The task is urgent because the object we need you to retrieve is due to be auctioned, secretly of course, sometime in the next few days. The task is of absolute importance because the object is the one we refer to as *SS*.'

'Dear God!' Raphael's heart pounded. He had been right, there was only one missing object that could be defined as absolute. The search for it had begun as soon as the Second World War ended and now, perhaps, there was the chance of completion. 'How sure are you?'

'Sure enough to assign our most experienced and successful operative.'

'To bring this home would be...' Raphael's voice trailed off. He couldn't find the words.

'It would be to return the secret Heart to Mother Church.' The bald man said it for him. 'It would be the ultimate demonstration of your faith and ability.'

'I... I am honoured to accept the responsibility,' Raphael felt a sudden pressure squeezing his chest. 'Honoured and humbled.'

'As you should be.' The bald man shifted in his chair. 'There can be no errors and, as ever, there can be nothing that attracts media attention. Retrieve this most precious of all objects and respond to those who currently possess it with terminal efficiency.'

'Of course.' Raphael nodded slowly.

Terminal efficiency.

The death sentence.

It had been demanded many times in the past for those who trafficked in far less significant objects, so it came as no surprise now.

Pietro had taught from the very beginning that the work of an MK operative involved both retrieval and punishment. The young Raphael had accepted that. He trusted in the wisdom of his seniors; he had been secure in his faith. Increasingly, though, he had found himself struggling with the role of executioner. The ever-increasing time he was spending alone, deep in meditation, was bringing questions and doubts to the surface. How could the most holy of men order the deaths of others? How could the love of God be expressed by such violence?

'Remember the very roots of your calling and the infinite goodness you serve,' the bald man said suddenly. 'St Peter created what we have long called the Mystiko Kataskopos because he knew that, for the Church to survive and grow, it needed a means of protecting itself. Since then men like you – men of faith, men who act – have done this job admirably. You know the history of the MK. You know the vital role it plays. Now you are entrusted with the most important of all tasks. I know God will sharpen your mind and strengthen your hand. Contact me only when it is done. Here is all the information you need.'

The bald man removed a brown, sealed envelope from his inside jacket pocket and placed it on the table. He stood abruptly and left without saying another word.

Raphael sat, unmoving, for several minutes. When he finally reached out for the envelope his hand was shaking.

6

The next day he took an early morning East Midlands train to St Pancras International station, London. The journey took just over one hundred minutes. He travelled first class. He meditated most the way, feeling the steady rhythm of his heart. He chose his favourite meditation, using the word *Abba* – the Aramaic word for Father – as a silent mantra, repeating the first syllable on the in-breath and the second syllable on the out. Around him businessmen and women prepared for their meetings.

On arrival Raphael merged with the crowd heading down to the Underground. He took the Piccadilly Line to Green Park and made the two-minute walk into Dover Street, threading his way through the lines of pedestrians until he reached the Georgian building that was to be his temporary home. The apartment was at the top. Raphael chose the stairs rather than the lift and ran up them, imagining that Mia was ahead of him. His work often led him into the world's major cities; none held the appeal of the Derbyshire hills.

The apartment had grand, double-heighted entrance doors

that opened to reveal a large open-plan living and dining room, a separate kitchen and two double bedrooms both ensuite. It was the sort of safe house, worth millions, that only the Church would provide.

Raphael had always felt uncomfortable staying in such places. He didn't need luxury in order to accomplish his missions. Originally he had believed it to be a deliberate test, his handler's way of seeing if he could be easily distracted; if material possessions held any sway over him. That belief, though, had long since gone. Now he was more inclined to accept that the Church was simply shrewd in its investments.

Raphael chose the bedroom nearest to the doors and placed his rucksack on the bed. He crossed to the window and looked out over the rooftops and down at the street below. Even through the soles of his Nike trainers he could feel the thick pile of the carpet beneath his feet. He was reminded of the unblemished soles of his handler's shoes. He wondered if he had ever undertaken a mission, if he had ever ended an encounter with terminal efficiency. Raphael turned his back on the view and went into the kitchen. He poured himself a glass of water, took the notes he had been given out of his jacket pocket, and sat at the table to read them. He had already been through them a dozen times. He knew all the facts by heart. This time he would use them as a meditative tool, looking at the words and images as if they were a holy text or sacred art. Silent, thoughtless observation was the final step in his preparation. It could last for hours.

Today it did. When Raphael left the flat, the Autumn sun was already weak in the sky. Raphael nodded with satisfaction. Urgency did not equate to unnecessary haste. Timing was everything. And this was the time to begin. He set off at a brisk pace. His target was less than a ten-minute walk away. It was a penthouse apartment that made his accommodation look decidedly second-rate.

Raphael walked northwest on Dover Street before turning left onto Hay Hill and then right into Berkeley Square. He ignored the gardens and the large trees, the architecture, the tourists and the suited executives. He kept his head low. He knew the route. His sense of purpose was stronger than it had ever been. To discover and return the object known as *SS* would be the ultimate act of service; to see and actually hold it, an experience greater than any he could imagine.

Raphael turned southwest out of Berkeley Square onto Hill Street. It was lined with what had once been individual houses and were now mostly grand apartments. He passed the Coach and Horses pub and kept walking until he was level with the building topped by the penthouse he intended to search.

He had been provided with keys that guaranteed him entry. According to his notes the penthouse was currently uninhabited, and no security personnel were present. He found it hard to believe that an object as precious as the SS could be there unprotected. He dealt with his uncertainty by reminding himself that, often, the best way to hide something was in plain sight, encouraging the assumption that, because there was no protection, there was nothing of value present.

What was the lesson Pietro had shared? Oh yes. It was based on the words of the Middle Eastern mystic Epiah Khan.

Everything has to be somewhere.

So maybe the most precious of all Christian objects was here, unguarded, in a Mayfair penthouse. Maybe his most important mission was also going to be his easiest.

Raphael resisted the temptation to slow his pace. His level of awareness was now at its most acute. He would see everything he needed in the few seconds it took to pass the building.

And he did.

She was standing on the other side of the road, a woman in her early thirties with short blond hair and green eyes. She was wearing blue jeans and a brown leather bomber jacket. She had red-coloured trainers on her feet. She was pretending to speak on her phone.

Her eyes betrayed her; they were too deliberately focused on the same building that he was interested in. The unnecessary tension in her body confirmed the falsehood. If, like him, she was a professional, then she had been poorly trained.

Raphael continued down the street without hesitation. As far as he could tell, the woman was working alone. There was no sign of accomplices in nearby cars, at windows or on the pavement. Raphael walked a hundred metres without once glancing back. Then he crossed the road, using his peripheral vision to check for her whereabouts. She hadn't moved. She was still engaged in her imaginary phone conversation. She was clearly unaware of him.

Raphael walked towards her. He kept close to the edge of the pavement, letting his arms swing more than usual, giving her every opportunity to notice him. Finally she did, one quick glance followed by the irresistible double take. Raphael stared back. The woman pulled her gaze away, her phone hand dropping from her face. Her cheeks coloured. When they were only ten metres apart Raphael clapped his hands together once, loudly. She glanced again automatically, realised he was still staring and looked down quickly at her phone.

Raphael passed in front of her, looking deliberately at the building opposite, tilting his head up to make it clear he was looking at the penthouse. He took a dozen steps before looking back over his shoulder. Now she was watching him. He made sure she saw his cold, hard smile. Then he continued along the street and turned into the Coach and Horses.

The pub seemed at odds with its environs. The rich, dark wood, the feature fireplace, the brass foot rail along the bar, all suggested a place that was hanging on to its history and heritage; a place that wasn't for converting. Raphael ordered tonic water with ice and lemon and positioned himself at a dark brown wooden table facing the bar. He guessed he wouldn't have long to wait. Amateurs and incompetent professionals could be drawn out as easily as moths to a flame.

He took a sip of his drink and sat back against the brown leather upholstery. He inhaled deeply and felt the shoulder sheath and the six-inch blade it contained snug beneath his jacket. He thought instinctively of the last person he had killed.

It had been a South American man in possession of Caravaggio's lost masterpiece, The Nativity with St Francis and St Lawrence. The painting, also known as The Adoration, had been stolen originally in 1969. The South American was believed to have purchased it from a member of the Sicilian mafia. Raphael had said a prayer over his dead body, just as he had all the others.

They had all been men, all violent criminals who were enemies of the Church. Each of them would have ended his life without hesitation if he hadn't been more skilled and more committed. The world was undoubtedly a safer place without them. Yet, increasingly, their ghosts seemed to haunt him.

His handler's question echoed suddenly:

Have you, I wonder, kept count of the many precious things returned by your own hands?

The truthful answer, the one he could never share, was:

I don't count the precious things I have returned; I count only the lives I have taken.

Raphael shifted uncomfortably in his seat. Please God the *SS* was, indeed, hidden unprotected in plain sight and he would not have to kill again.

The pub door opened. The woman entered. She bought herself an orange juice and joined him. Just as he had known she would. He watched her without blinking as she sat in front of him. The knife pressed against his chest.

7

'Who are you and why are you following me?' Her voice was a fierce whisper. He could sense the panic she was struggling to contain.

'I didn't follow you. You followed me,' Raphael said. 'I came in here for a drink; you could have gone anywhere else in the city. So actually, I should be asking who you are and why you're harassing me.'

'I'm not harassing you! And who I am is none of your business!'

'In which case, please leave me alone.' Raphael took another sip of his tonic water.

'You deliberately drew yourself to my attention. You know you did! I have the right to know why!' The woman forced herself to lean forwards, her palms flat on the table.

Raphael pretended to consider her demand. He nodded thoughtfully. 'Alright, I'll tell you,' he said finally. 'I am keeping an eye – a watchful eye, you might say – on the penthouse in the building you were studying. My friend owns the place and, whenever he's away, I watch over it for him. You were secretly taking photos of it, whilst acting as if you were making a phone call. That is suspicious behaviour. That's why I made sure you followed me here. I want to know why you are so interested in my friend's home.'

The woman sat back. Her eyes widened. 'You know the owner?'

'Sir Desmond Swann. Yes. I once worked for him in a certain capacity.'

'Some form of security, I should bet.'

Raphael shrugged, unblinking, letting the silence build. Only a few seconds passed before the woman spoke again. Her voice was faster this time.

'He's a billionaire, isn't he? I read he's some sort of long-distance relation of the Royal family. You must know that, of course. If you worked for him in security you must know a hell of a lot more, too. God alone knows what sort of things you've done if you've taken money off a man like that.' She pushed the orange juice away from her. 'Behind Swann's rich, upper-class façade with his network of Lords and Ladies, politicians and business leaders, there's a stinking cesspool of abuse and violence and death. It's well hidden, of course. And those few who do know about it are more than happy to pretend they don't. It pays to keep on the right side of a corrupt billionaire, doesn't it? That's what you've obviously done. Protected his interests and, no doubt, got your hands dirty for whatever rewards he's given you. So, what are you going to do now – try to take my phone off me?'

'No. I'm more interested in whatever harm Desmond Swann has caused you, than whatever might be on your phone.' Raphael let his face soften for the first time. 'I want to know why you hate this man so much.'

'Assessing the level of threat that I pose, are you?' She arched an eyebrow, her tone scornful.

'If I am, it's only the level of threat you might be posing to yourself.' He smiled. 'I didn't tell you how I worked for him; it was you who presumed the worst. You did it so easily you must have good reason to. So, if I assure you that I have never been a part of Sir Desmond Swann's security, and I have never carried out any of the illegal acts you think he is ultimately responsible for, will you please tell me what he's done to you?'

She looked him in the eyes. He saw a mixture of doubt, confusion and a faint glimmer of hope. He waited for her to organise her response. 'Before I tell you anything, I need to know what you actually did when you worked for him,' she said.

'Nothing at all. I lied to you. I just needed to feed you something in the hope of getting an insight into your motives.' He smiled again. 'Not the best way of gaining trust I appreciate that, but it wasn't harmful and it did the trick – up to a point, anyway.'

She frowned, shaking her head as she tried to make sense of what she had heard. 'Then why did my behaviour matter so much to you? What was it ...' Her voice trailed off as a possibility dawned. 'You're some type of detective, aren't you? Maybe even a member of a special unit? You noticed me because you're investigating Swann! Is that it?'

'I'm not at liberty to comment.' Raphael pushed his glass to one side. 'What I can tell you is that if Desmond Swann is as corrupt as you say, he would be a person of extreme interest to myself and the organisation I represent. And you would have been putting yourself at considerable risk by showing such an obvious interest in his property.'

'He is as corrupt as I said. Actually, I'm sure he's a damn sight worse. And if you're being honest with me now, you are obviously involved in law enforcement.'

Raphael inclined his head. 'It's time for you to tell me your story. All of it. Despite everything you've said, I'm still afraid that you don't understand what you are getting yourself mixed up in.

So, please, share everything. I am one of the good guys. I promise.'

He watched her relax. He knew she was going to talk. He could see that she needed to. His heart beat strongly against the hidden knife. The same thought kept pounding in the back of his mind.

I've never had to kill a woman before.

8

'My name is Catherine Morgan. Everyone knows me as Cat.' She almost offered her hand but stopped herself. She continued quickly. 'I'm a Detective Constable in the Metropolitan Police. Policing is the family career. It's what I wanted to do from an early age. My dad and both of his brothers wore the uniform. My brother, Peter, he er...' Her voice trembled. She looked down for a moment before regaining control. 'He was a few years older than me. He was my best friend. He got into the Force before I did. He performed brilliantly right from the very beginning, but wearing a uniform was never going to be enough for him.

'So, as soon as he could, he got himself into a different type of policing – anti-terrorism, undercover stuff. Obviously he couldn't tell me much about it, but it was clear that he loved what he was doing. He used to say there were few people in life who ever truly found their vocation and that he was forever grateful that he had. He said if you loved and believed in the work you were doing, you would always find peace, even if things became challenging.'

Cat paused briefly and looked directly at Raphael. 'Do you agree with that? Is what you do your vocation?'

'Yes,' he said it automatically. There was nothing else he could say, even though something inside him twisted and pulled as he spoke. He shifted the conversation back to her. 'What happened to Peter?'

She blanched and inhaled deeply. 'He was killed. Murdered. His body was found in a waste dump. It had been transported there and left. Someone was making a very deliberate point. They were saying my brother was a piece of trash.'

'I'm very sorry.' Raphael let himself feel her loss before continuing. 'Was it work-related?'

'Of course it was!' Cat's anger flared. 'We had a few too many beers one night and Peter let slip that he was monitoring Sir Desmond Swann. There was reason to believe that, beyond the drugs, prostitution and people trafficking, he was also supplying arms to various terrorist groups. Peter was part of a small team assigned to observing and recording what Swann was up to. He told me he'd developed a contact that had vital information – enough to prove Swann's guilt. I think it was all a ploy. I think Peter was lured into a trap and killed.' Tears began to run down her face. 'According to the autopsy report, Peter was knocked unconscious and then had his throat cut. It was a clinical, deliberate killing. After that, all traces of Swann's involvement in illegal arms trading disappeared.'

'And there are always more immediate threats for anti-terrorist teams to focus on.'

'Absolutely.' Cat wiped the tears away. 'That's part of the tragedy of it all, isn't it? Whatever happens today, we have to be ready for something worse that might happen tomorrow. There is no respite. There is no such thing as a victory. This is a conflict made up of never-ending challenges. We don't get rewarded for our victories. In fact, they never even get a mention. No, the politicians and the media are all silent until we make a mistake or miss a signal and members of the public die as a consequence. Then there's the enquiry and the news reports and the call for people to be sacked or sued.

'There was no enquiry or outcry when Peter had his throat sliced open so viciously his head was almost severed. That was kept quiet because, somehow, our leaders have decided that's the most appropriate response. Let's not tell the world that a brave, loving undercover police officer lost his life trying to keep us safe. Instead let's leave a billionaire knight to carry on doing whatever he likes and pretend that the greatest threat to our liberty and way of life comes from strangers living abroad!'

Raphael waited until her emotion was under control. 'The sacrifices no one ever hears of,' he said. 'They're the greatest sacrifices of all, and the most difficult to bear for those few who know about them.' He sighed. 'I still don't why you were outside Swann's penthouse. I'm guessing you weren't there representing the Met?'

'No,' Cat shook her head. 'Peter died three months ago. I've been on sick leave ever since. It's only in the last few days that I've felt strong enough to start doing what needs to be done.'

'And that is?'

'Get enough evidence to put Swann away for the rest of his life.'

'Do you think you've got the skills and the ability to do that?' He asked the question gently.

The anger shone in her eyes. 'Someone has to do something! He was my brother and he died doing what our country needed him to do! If we don't have enough officers to ensure he gets justice, then I need to do it!'

'I understand that. Maybe now, though, because you've met me and you realise that Swann is still under investigation, you can back off and focus on your own and your family's recovery?'

'That isn't possible.'

'Why not?'

'Because, regardless of who you work for, you could get pulled off this case and onto another at any time. It's like you said, more immediate threats can arise in an instant and they become the priority. I know this sounds horrible, but there is nothing more important to me than getting my brother's killer punished.'

'He is going to be punished, I promise you that.' Raphael remembered the South American. 'And I can't help but think that Peter would want you to keep yourself safe; your family shouldn't have to risk another loss.'

'I owe it to Peter. The only way I'm going to be able to live my life again is by doing this first. Swann is too rich, too well connected and too far removed from the actual crimes his people commit for the police ever to get enough evidence against him. And even if you were able to charge him with something, it wouldn't stick. He's got an army of lawyers and an even bigger army of villains who'll do anything he says. Apart from that he probably owns half the judges in the land.'

'Just because bad things happen, it doesn't mean the world is essentially a bad place. Just because some people do bad things, it doesn't mean that people are essentially bad. The worst of times are when we need to have the most faith. Right now, you need to have faith in me. You need to go home.'

'Christ! You sound more like a vicar than an undercover detective!' Cat spat the words out, her right hand bunching into a fist. 'Maybe you're the one who's not cut out for this?'

Raphael watched her instinctively pull her feet back under her stool. He decided that if she lashed out, he would accept the strike. He waited, silent and still. Her rage dissipated. Her hand relaxed. Her shoulders slumped. Suddenly she was close to tears.

'He didn't deserve to die,' she said.

'No, he didn't.'

It was the simple truth. No less heartbreaking for all that. And the other equally simple truth was that he only ever worked alone, undetected and unknown. Now, Cat knew he was here. She knew his face, even if she didn't know his name. Now he had questions to answer and a decision to make. If he couldn't persuade her to walk away – if he couldn't be completely sure that she would – he was left with only one, lethal alternative. Could he, if necessary, carry it out? Could he justify such an act even for the most important mission of his life?

His handler's voice filled his mind.

To return the secret Heart to Mother Church would be the ultimate demonstration of your faith and ability.

Raphael shook the memory away.

Cat had regained her self-control. Before Raphael could speak, she said, 'I'm not going anywhere. Even if you call in some of your colleagues to have me removed, I'll be right back. You haven't got the manpower to have me monitored twenty-four seven, and you certainly won't lock me up. So, Mr Detective whose name I still don't know, you've either got to leave me alone to do my own thing or agree to let me work with you. What's it going to be?'

He looked past her, over her shoulders. Sunlight filtered in through the windows. Outside the city rushed around them. He retreated to the meditative place at the back of his brain. His heart slowed automatically. He knew what he had to do. She reminded him too much of Gemma for him to do anything else.

'You are going to follow my instructions at all times and without question,' he said. 'Is that clear?'

Cat smiled. 'Yes, boss.' She raised her glass in salute. He couldn't stop himself from following suit.

9

They arrived back at the expensive safe house thirty minutes later. Cat had already told him she felt a connection between them, created no doubt because they shared a common purpose. He had wondered more than once if his relationship with Gemma had become a handicap. Regardless, he opened the grand entrance doors and invited her inside.

'Oh my God!' Cat pivoted three hundred and sixty degrees as she took in the expansive living and dining space. 'How can you afford a place like this?'

'I have friends in high places.' Raphael led the way to the second bedroom. 'This is yours,' he said, 'but only until we finish here. When I go, so do you.'

'You don't need to tell me that,' she chided.

'I need to tell you all of the rules. And you need to do precisely as I tell you. That's the deal, remember?'

'It's impossible to forget! You've told me ten times at least since I offered to help you.'

'You didn't offer to help. I agreed to let you join in. I'm the professional here. You're the under-trained policewoman who doesn't know how to carry out surveillance without being obvious, and who has no idea of the risk she's taking.'

'My brother was murdered!' She snapped.

'In part, that's why I've allowed you to be here,' Raphael kept his voice under control. 'However you weren't there when it happened, were you? Let's be honest – and we need to be if we are going to be successful together – I doubt that you've experienced any significant violence, let alone seen anyone killed up close and personal. Isn't that true?'

'I don't see what that has to do with anything.' Cat turned away from him.

'We're heading into a potentially violent situation and neither of us can know how you will respond if things turn ugly.'

She spun back to face him. 'And I suppose you know exactly how you will respond? You're an expert at violence and death, are you?'

'I've seen more than my fair share,' he said quietly. 'It goes with my job.'

Cat shook her head as her emotions shifted. 'How do you deal with it?' She asked.

'I believe in the righteousness of my cause,' he said, 'and I accept that violence and death are an inevitable part of life.'

'You're sounding like a vicar again.' Cat smiled. 'Do you really think such things are inevitable?'

Raphael shrugged. 'Every day on this planet there is the violence of birth and the violence of death. It's an integral part of nature. When you add on to that the fact that some human beings are prepared to break the law and commit heinous crimes in pursuit of power and wealth, then I'd say it becomes inevitable on many levels.'

'Are you ever going to tell me which part of the police force or which national security department you belong to?'

'No. For all sorts of reasons, the less you know about me the better things are for both of us. Now, I'm going into my room to do some final planning. I'll probably be a couple of hours. I suggest you get some rest if you can. It's going to be a busy night.'

Raphael closed her bedroom door as he left. He doubted that she would manage to sleep, but then he had no intention of spending any more time planning. That had been done before he had even walked along Hill Street. At this stage in the proceedings, before he made his first obvious move against his target, he needed to meditate.

He chose to sit, cross-legged on the floor at the foot of his bed. He brought his hands together and closed his eyes. It took only one second for his thoughts to stop. He surrendered to the state completely, disappearing in the vast emptiness that seemed to surround and sweep through him. Within moments he was barely aware of his own existence. Only the slow, rhythmic beating of his heart remained, and even that felt as if it belonged elsewhere.

He couldn't know how long he remained that way, but the emptiness was disrupted suddenly by the image of the road. This time it appeared so abruptly his body jerked backwards against the bed. The shock seemed to improve the clarity of the vision. It was a deserted country road, lined with trees and bushes. It was narrow, twisting ahead of him this way and that. He had the sense that he was standing on it. His instinct was to take a step, to accept the invitation it offered. Raphael felt his right foot twitch and at once the image disappeared and his eyes opened.

It was 8pm. He had been there longer than he had intended. His conscious mind wanted him to sit still and consider what the vision meant. Instead he went into the living room. Cat was sat at the dining room table, staring at something on her mobile phone.

'You haven't made or received any calls, have you?' His voice was louder than he meant it to be.

'You told me not to and I'm following orders.' She looked up at him. 'You also said that you needed a couple of hours. I was beginning to think you'd snuck out without telling me.'

'As you can see, I hadn't.' Raphael poured himself a glass of water. 'Do you want a drink?'

'No. I want to know what the plan is.'

He sat down opposite her. 'It's simple. We return to the penthouse, double-check that it's empty and unguarded and let ourselves in as if we have done it a hundred times before. Once we are inside and the alarm is off, I'll tell you precisely what sort of things to look for and how to do it. We are going to work on the principle that we have limited time in the place – I'll tell you how long once we are inside – so we need to be thorough and efficient. When our time is up, we leave. If we find what we need ahead of time, we leave. If I suddenly tell you we have to get out—'

'—we leave,' Cat finished the sentence for him. 'Isn't that just a bit too simple?'

'No. There are two kinds of simple in my line of work. There is the simplicity of the unprepared, over-confident amateur who has done no in-depth preparation and has limited skills.' Raphael looked at her pointedly. 'Then there is the streamlined, well-planned simplicity of the expert who, because of their ability and experience make things seems easy.'

'And you're the streamlined expert?'

'Obviously.' Raphael patted his stomach.

Cat smiled despite herself. 'So you checked out Swann's penthouse before today?'

'Someone did.'

'Will that someone be watching us tonight?'

'No. We are on our own. Too many unknown faces, too much

unusual behaviour, can attract the attention of neighbours. The last thing we want to do is attract attention. We need to fit in. So when we leave here we are going to walk together as if we don't have a care in the world and we've known each other forever.'

'We are not going to pretend we are lovers!'

'No,' he smiled. 'We are definitely not going to do that.' Raphael glanced at his watch, walked over to the window and looked down at the busy street. Although they were only a few hundred metres away from the world-famous Ritz hotel, there were still people on the pavement offering passers-by every kind of service, from drugs to sex. There would be even more of them as the night turned into the early hours of the morning. He intended to be back in the apartment well before then.

'We will leave here in ten minutes,' he said. 'If anyone approaches us as we walk, avoid looking at them, keep your head down and let me communicate however I choose. We don't want to be slowed down, distracted or remembered. And if, at any point, anything goes wrong and I tell you to jump, make sure you do.'

'Here you go again,' Cat sighed. 'I was the high jump champion at school, so you don't need to worry about me.'

'I'm not worrying about you, I'm worrying about the success of my mission.' Raphael hardened his face as he spoke. He couldn't help but think that Gemma would have seen right through it.

10

The walk back to Swann's penthouse passed without incident. He ensured they moved with the brusque confidence of a local couple best left alone. He kept Cat on the inside, away from the road, with his left hand gently but firmly on her right elbow. For her part, she accepted his lead without question and matched him pace for pace. Only when they turned into Hill Street did he feel her tense slightly.

'Look at me and smile,' he said.

'What?'

'Look at me, think of something that makes you happy, and smile.'

'I don't do happiness anymore.'

'I'd realised that.'

'So why did you ask me to?'

'I just needed to interrupt the mood you were getting into. If the security situation has changed, we need to be able to walk past the penthouse without being noticed.'

'Walk past it?'

'If someone is standing guard we'll hardly be able to talk our way in, will we? And I hope you don't think I'd simply demolish them with some slick martial arts moves.'

'Could you?'

Raphael shrugged. 'We'll never know. Look, the place is just as we left it.'

They turned off the pavement. The keys were in his hand before they reached the impressive front door. Seconds later they were inside.

'Keep your gloves on at all times,' Raphael said. They were both wearing thin, leather gloves. He had insisted they wear them since leaving the safe house. 'We're going to take the stairs, not the lift.'

He moved without waiting for a reply.

She followed. They saw no one. They didn't speak again until they had entered the penthouse.

'Jesus Christ!' Cat stared at the grand entrance hall. 'This feels more like a mansion than a flat!'

'And this is just his London home.' Raphael locked the doors behind them. 'Follow me.' He led the way into the spacious lounge. 'The penthouse is over three floors,' he said. 'Here we've got the lounge, a dining room, an entertainment suite and a kitchen. Above us there are three double-bedrooms, all en-suite and a large, very private roof terrace. I'm going to start searching upstairs. You search down here.'

'And if I find anything at all that might be related to criminal activity I'll call you.'

'Yes, just as we agreed. This isn't the time or the place for you to do your own thing. Right?'

'Right.'

'And avoid being distracted by all the expensive, shiny things,' he said as he left the room.

Cat glared at his back and stabbed the upraised middle finger of her right hand in the air. Her heart was pounding. 'I have to focus,' she told herself when he had disappeared. 'I can't afford to behave like the grieving sister.'

She decided to begin with the ornate chest of drawers in the furthest corner of the room. Thankfully it was unlocked. Cat took a deep breath and began searching.

Raphael went straight to the master bedroom. It was at least five times the size of the monastic cell he had called home for three years. He couldn't imagine how much the carpet and the furnishings cost. However, it was the walls he was most interested in, especially behind the paintings and at the back of the built-in wardrobes.

If the *SS* was hidden here it would be in a safe, fastened securely into either a wall or the floor. He guessed it was most likely to be in a wall. Raphael couldn't believe that anyone would store such a holy object underfoot.

He hadn't told Cat anything about his real mission or role. During their time together in the safe house she had tried several times to find out more, but he had managed to satisfy her curiosity without adding any significant details. 'When you are seeking to be unknown, avoid too many details,' Pietro had said. 'The Devil lives there and he will find you out.'

It hadn't just been a lesson about how to be an agent for the Mystiko Kataskopos, it was also a reminder of how a monk should regard possessions. There could only be too many, never too few. The Devil waited, disguised, in the details of ownership.

Raphael worked his way round the room with clinical haste. Despite his experience and very deliberate focus, he couldn't help but feel a mix of emotions pulsing through his body. Any moment now he could discover the hiding place of the most important religious object on the planet. He could become the first member of the Church for generations to hold it. He could be one of only a few in history who ever had!

Raphael paused briefly and calmed his breathing. Then he

stepped into the large, walk-in wardrobe. It was lined on both sides with expensive suits, jackets and trousers. A full-length mirror dominated the end wall. Raphael was drawn towards it. He studied the screws, one in each corner, holding it in place. Something about them was wrong. He couldn't see what exactly, but his instinct was urging him to explore. He did.

He took a penknife out of his jeans pocket and placed the tip into the groove of the top right-hand screw. It turned easily. So did the others. It took him less than two minutes to release the mirror from the wall.

The safe was positioned at head height. Raphael frowned when he saw it. He knew the brand. He knew the quality. It was fire-resistant and virtually indestructible. It had a half-inch thick steel door and a high security electronic keypad lock. It provided a level of challenge that would have defeated most. But not Raphael. Given time he could open this safe, just as he could any other. No, it wasn't the defensive capability that made him frown. Rather, it was the size.

The safe he was looking at measured sixteen inches by nineteen inches and was less than fourteen inches deep. He doubted if it could contain the object he was here for. Despite that, he would still have to check. First, though, he would go through the other bedrooms to see if there was a larger version elsewhere. With the decision made, Raphael turned to go into the nearest room.

It was then Cat began screaming.

11

He raced downstairs. Two men were in the lounge. They were large, muscular and dressed in black. Cat had backed into a corner and was holding a vase in both hands as if to strike out with it. The man nearest the lounge door glanced over his shoulder and saw Raphael. He turned to face him.

Raphael pulled his right fist back, telegraphing the punch. The man automatically brought his left forearm up as a cover and angled to his right, away from the impending strike. Raphael had never intended to throw it. His raised right fist was designed to draw the man into line for a kick with his left foot. He delivered it mid-stride. It benefited from both his forward momentum and his opponent's. It struck the centre of the man's pelvis, breaking the bone in half. The man screamed as his hips buckled inwards and he collapsed onto the luxurious carpet.

Raphael continued past the fallen man, closing in on the other. He was met with a flurry of punches targeting his face and throat. He raised both elbows, timing his move so well the man couldn't stop his fists from thudding into them. Bones in his hands cracked and his arms dropped momentarily. Raphael stamped the sole of his right foot through the man's left knee.

His head came forwards and down. Raphael bounced his foot off the floor and smashed his right knee into the down-coming face. He felt the man's nose and cheekbones shatter. As the body fell he looked at Cat.

She was staring at him, open-mouthed and terrified. She was clutching the vase now as if it were a protective blanket.

'We have to leave,' he said.

She shook her head in disbelief. She didn't move. 'They might not be alone,' he said. 'And even if they are, others will follow quickly once they don't report back.'

'What... What did you just do?' Her voice was hollow.

She gestured vaguely towards the bodies.

He knew she was in shock. He wondered how difficult it would be to get her swiftly and safely back to their flat. 'I neutralised them to save you,' he replied. 'I kept us safe – for the moment. C'mon, we have to go.'

Cat pointed. 'There's blood on your clothing.'

'It's dark now,' he said. 'It's unlikely anyone will notice.'

'You could have killed them!' She screamed. 'I don't care if people see the blood! You were like an animal!'

'I didn't kill them because I chose not to.' He took a step towards her. 'And you're right, some animals are willing to kill to protect those in their care.'

'I'm not in your care!'

Raphael looked at her and the question resurfaced.

Have I made a mistake in letting her live?

The memory of Gemma's last training session with Falco filled his mind. He thought then of the many female disciples of Christ; how Jesus seemed more relaxed at the home of Mary and Martha, the sisters of Lazarus, than anywhere else.

The answer was obvious. Cat was a woman who was out of her depth; she needed saving not drowning.

'Remember our deal?' He asked. 'You can't do your own

thing. You have to trust me. That's the only way we have a chance of bringing Swann to justice and honouring your brother.'

She looked him in the eyes. He kept talking.

'Those men work for Swann. Somehow they were alerted to our presence. Someone who works for Swann killed Peter. I guarantee you these two wouldn't have let us walk away. If we are going to make sure their colleagues don't succeed where they failed, we have to get out of here. Now!'

Cat nodded slowly.

'Look at the door,' Raphael said, 'and walk towards it. Remember the splendour of the entrance hall and focus only on that.'

Cat's first steps were slow, her legs shaking.

'That's great!' He encouraged. 'Each step will make you stronger.'

They did.

By the time they were back on the street some colour had returned to her cheeks. Raphael steered her along the pavement, gradually increasing their pace, talking continuously until she began to reply. They were in the safe house less than thirty minutes after he had broken the face of the second attacker. He made a point of locking the doors.

'Are we safe now?' She asked.

Raphael shrugged. 'Do you feel safe?'

'No. I don't feel safe from them, and I don't feel safe from you.'

He sat down on one of the two settees. She remained standing.

'I'm not your enemy,' he said.

'You were like a mad dog!' She snapped back.

'No. Mad dogs are sick and untrained. I'm neither.'

'Why haven't you called someone to report back?'

'There hasn't been much time for that, has there?'

'So are you going to do it now?'

'No.'

'Why not?'

'Because that isn't how I'm expected to operate. When I'm released on a task I only report back when I have a result.'

'Peter wasn't allowed to do that when he was undercover.'

'Peter was a relative beginner. I'm not. Neither am I required to follow the same rules he was.'

'Why?'

'Because different... departments have different protocols.'

'But if you can't contact your superior, how do you get help if you need it?'

'Usually I don't need help. On the odd occasion that I have, there is always a knowledgeable contact at an agreed meeting place. I simply turn up there at a certain time if there's something I need. That's part of how we operate, part of our planning. There are always several layers.'

'But what if you can't get to that meeting place?'

'Then I have to resolve the problem myself. Although on this occasion I've also got you to rely on.'

'That sounds like sarcasm.'

'It was meant as a matter of fact, as a reminder. Whilst I do need you to follow my lead, I need you to do so actively. We almost certainly haven't finished fighting them yet, and I don't want to have to fight you as well.'

'Of course I'm sorry.' Cat sat on the settee opposite him. 'How does it feel?'

'How does what feel?'

'Causing that much harm to another human being.'

He sighed. 'You can't do it well if you don't really want to. That's the truth. I need a powerful reason – a cause – that's bigger than either them or me. When I have that reason I'm fully prepared and willing to do whatever I have to.'

'So you find it easy?'

'I'm physically and mentally very well trained.'

'That was avoidance disguised as an answer.'

'Yes.' He nodded.

'So what's the real answer?'

Raphael looked up at the ceiling, he recalled his handler in the bar at The Cavendish Hotel. The real answer was,

I'm finding it more and more difficult and I'm scared of where this particular task might lead.

Instead he said, 'I don't have the luxury of considering a real answer. I have too many important things to do to spend time thinking about myself.'

'I'm not sure if that sounds noble or tragic.'

'It doesn't matter how it sounds, it doesn't feel either.' He forced a smile.

She didn't recognise the effort it took and smiled back.

Then her face clouded. 'Are you lonely?'

'No,' this time the answer was both honest and easy. 'I can't remember a time I've ever felt lonely.'

'Do you have a family?'

'In a manner of speaking.'

'What the hell does that mean?'

'It means the interview is over.' He stood up. 'The fact that we were interrupted means they are onto us already. The fact they sent only two run-of-the-mill heavies means they don't know who I am. I doubt they'll make that mistake again.'

'But it was enough to stop us finding anything, and they're bound to increase security on the place now.'

'So we have to change our plan.'

'*Our* plan?'

'OK. I have to change my plan. Then I will tell you about it.'

Cat turned her head away from him. 'The violence made me think of Peter's death,' she said.

'Everything we do takes us a step closer to honouring his memory and validating his life.'

'Even when there's blood on your clothes?'

'Yes. Even if it was our blood.'

Raphael walked back to the window. He looked out. On the opposite side of the road a shaven-headed man wearing black jeans and a black bomber jacket was looking up at the flat. He made no attempt to turn away when he saw Raphael. Both men held their gaze. Neither blinked. Raphael counted his heartbeat. Forty-three beats per minute.

'They've found us here, too,' he said, moving back to the settees.

'Swann's men?' Cat stood up.

'Yes.' Raphael tapped his hands together. Nothing was making sense. He had been as alert today as he had ever been. He hadn't been followed or observed at any time. As far as he knew they hadn't activated any security mechanisms at Swann's penthouse. No one had seen them return to their flat. Yet still someone was watching them.

'We have to leave,' he said. 'Follow me.'

He walked into the entrance hall. Cat was a pace behind.

'What do we do when we're outside?' She asked.

'We go into Green Park Tube Station.'

'Then?'

'We lose the guy who will be following us.'

'How?'

'You'll see.' They set off.

12

They eventually exited the tube at Lancaster Gate. The man who was tailing them had been lost somewhere, but Cat didn't know when or how. The look on Raphael's face told her not to ask. She stayed by his side as they walked onto Bayswater Road.

'Where are we going?' Cat touched his left upper arm as she spoke.

'Lancaster Gate Hotel,' he replied. 'I have a room reserved.'

'When did you do that?'

'I didn't, but it was done before I came to London.'

'One of the several layers?'

'Yes. It's best to have options already in place, so if things don't go as intended you have a "plan B" you can turn to automatically.'

'So everything you said about having to change your plan...?'

'Was true. The plan does have to change. The first few steps just happen to be in place already.'

'If you knew that, why didn't you tell me?'

'I wanted to see how you would respond.'

'You really are a bastard, do you know that?' Cat pulled away from him. 'I thought you trusted me?'

'I've only ever done this alone before. This is as new for me as it is for you.'

'So why did you agree to involve me?'

Because I couldn't kill you.

They walked in silence to the hotel. Raphael approached the reception desk alone. Cat didn't hear what he said. He rejoined her with a slight smile playing on his lips. They took the lift to the second floor. It was a twin room.

'I'm not sharing a bedroom with you,' Cat said.

'I'm not intending to spend much time here.' Raphael opened the bathroom door and looked inside. It was basic and clean.

Cat stood by one of the beds. 'What are you intending to do?'

'First of all, explore how they knew about us. There are several possibilities. One is that my people made a mistake or that one of them leaked information deliberately. That's impossible. The second option is that I missed something. I know I didn't. So that leaves us with the third option.'

'Which is?'

'You. You either made a mistake or you're working for them.'

'How dare you!' Cat rushed forwards and pushed his chest. He twisted slightly, nullifying the force. He didn't go backwards. She didn't want to touch him again.

'It was my brother they killed!' She shouted.

'That's why the most likely answer is that you made a mistake. If I spotted you that easily so could they.'

'But there was nobody there!'

'Maybe they were running occasional checks. I'm guessing you were there often and long enough to attract their attention.'

Cat flushed. 'I never thought about people checking from passing cars.'

'It could just as easily have been from a nearby flat. People can be persuaded to watch a neighbour's place and report in if they see anything suspicious. Most would think they were doing a good deed.'

Cat was silent for a moment. 'I've ruined it, haven't I?'

Raphael shook his head. 'No. You've just created a different avenue of opportunity.'

'Do you honestly see it like that?

'Sure. There isn't scope for any negativity when you're on the hunt.'

Cat laughed. 'Is that what we are – on the hunt?'

'Certainly. Our job is to search, and keep learning from feedback, until we find what we are looking for. Once we have retrieved it and passed it on, the work is done.'

'And along the way people might try to stop us?'

'As they already have. They're doing their job just as we're doing ours. The difference between us is two-fold. Firstly, our motivation is very different. We're driven by a cause, whilst they're driven by the need for money and power. They're selfish and uncaring, we are seeking to do what's best for society.'

'And the second difference?'

'I'm better trained than any of them.'

'Wow! There really are no doubts or negative beliefs in you!'

'I'm just being factual. As I said, we have to learn from feedback, and all the feedback I've received over many years is that I'm better at what I do than my opponents are.'

'How long did your training last?'

'It never ends.'

Raphael heard his own words and remembered the day Pietro died. They had all known his death was imminent. He had been diagnosed with bowel cancer two years earlier. He had refused medical treatment, changed his diet and increased his daily meditation. As his body weakened, the more insightful and powerful his teaching became. In the final weeks his eyes shone with a brightness and joy that belied the pain wracking his body.

Pietro died sometime during the night. He was found, slumped on his meditation cushion, at 6am by a fellow monk. Raphael had been the last person to speak to him.

'Breath is the greatest of all teachers,' Pietro had said. 'The final breath is the greatest of all lessons. I shall carry its learning with me when I move on...'

'What form does it take?' Cat's voice cut through his reverie.

'What?'

'Your training, what form does it take?'

'Oh. It's the usual mix.'

'You mean you're not going to tell me?'

'Something like that.'

'Would you have to kill me if you did?' Cat grinned.

Raphael forced a weak reply, trying to disguise the rush of emotion her question had released. 'No. No, of course not. I wouldn't kill you – someone else would.'

Cat giggled. 'And presumably my body would never be found?'

'Either that or your death would be made to look like an accident.'

The humour disappeared from her face. 'Peter didn't deserve to die,' she said. 'And I don't know why I just said what I did. I feel like I'm all over the place.'

'It's no surprise. If you're not prepared fully, this type of situation is guaranteed to mess with you psychologically and emotionally. The best thing you can do right now is acknowledge how it's affecting you and say what's on your mind.'

'Peter was a good person,' she said. 'He had a fiancée, dreams for the future. They sent him to do a job he wasn't prepared for. They knew the risks and still they sent him.'

'It was the role he chose,' Raphael said quietly.

'So why didn't they train him better? Why wasn't he as well trained as you?'

Raphael looked away. 'Sometimes there isn't an answer that can help,' he said.

'Is everyone in your department, or whatever it is, as good as you?'

He nodded. 'We are all very well trained. Inevitably, though, people have different levels of experience.'

'But they're not sent out like lambs to the slaughter! If my brother had been given your skills he would still be alive!'

'He might be. I'm not invulnerable. None of us are. We have our casualties, too.'

'Have you lost friends?'

'No matter how much we train we can't become perfect. We can't prevent loss.'

That had been Pietro's first lesson.

'I'm sorry.'

'Thank you.' He inhaled deeply. 'I have to go out now. You have to stay here. Stay in the room, don't venture down into the bar or reception.'

'Where are you going?'

'Not far away. I have to meet someone, the sort of knowledgeable contact I mentioned earlier. I know where he will be. He knows when to expect me. I don't want him, or anyone else for that matter, to find out about you.'

'Apart from the men who saw me in the penthouse?'

'What's done is done.' Raphael moved to the door. 'I'm going to this meeting precisely because the men saw us. I'm hoping my contact can help us get ahead in the game again. So, please, stay here.'

She nodded.

He closed the door behind him and made his way downstairs. When he stepped out into the Autumn night he paused and looked up at the sky. Stars sparkled as if nothing had changed. Yet every time he reviewed the events in Swann's penthouse, he kept coming to the same conclusion.

I should have killed them both.

Raphael set off to his meeting wondering for the first time if he was actually capable of succeeding in his task.

13

Raphael redirected his attention as he made his way onto Bayswater Road. The Swan pub was only a few hundred metres away. He couldn't help but appreciate the irony of the meeting place, given the man he was targeting.

His contact was waiting inside, sitting at a small, round table. Raphael joined him. He took a sip of the mineral water that had been bought for him.

His contact spoke first. He was a thin, poorly dressed man with several small, dark ink tattoos on the back of each hand. 'The legend,' he said, 'is that a famous highwayman called Claude Duval had his final drink in this pub on the way to his execution at Tyburn in 1670.'

'I decided long ago that drinking was bad for you.' Raphael had met this man once before. He had been unable to get straight down to business on that occasion, too.

'The tradition was to stop off at a pub en route so that the prisoner could have a beer. They reckon that's how we got the phrase "one for the road". It originally meant the last drink before going to your death. And when the condemned man left the pub and was returned to the carriage he was said to be "on the wagon", meaning he would never drink again.' The man grinned. 'From what I've heard, you've been on the wagon forever.'

'We're all journeying towards our death.' Raphael was expressionless. 'But not today, God willing.' He took another sip of water. 'So what do you have for me about our friend's operation in the city?'

The man took a large swallow of his beer before replying. 'The main players have been in place for some time. Their reputations are established and their processes are slick. The guy in charge is known as Mad Eddie. People who work for him follow his rules precisely. People who owe him pay with interest, and they do it quickly. He's the really dangerous sort. He has a brain but he doesn't have a conscience. Stop Mad Eddie and you throw everything into confusion, at least for a while.'

'Where is he based?'

'He operates out of a bar he owns in St James, just off Jermyn Street. He's a big guy, greying, shaven-headed, with an unfinished tattoo of a Samurai on his left upper arm. If you're thinking of paying him a visit, I've been assured that the security cameras behind the bar don't work, they're just for show. The ones outside are functional, though. So make sure your keep your head down as you approach the place and when you leave.'

'OK.' Raphael shifted in his chair. 'So you think it's Mad Eddie who sent the men after us?'

'Whether or not he ordered them it's impossible to say, but they wouldn't have been there without him knowing about it.' The man took another large gulp of his beer. 'What, er, did you do to them, if you don't mind me asking? I guess one way or another you sent them to meet their Maker?'

'Is that what you believe?'

'What, that you, er –'

'That we have a Maker.'

84

'Never given it any consideration really, plenty of time for that when there's no more time for beer.' The man drained his glass. 'So what did you do to them?'

'I left them alive.'

'What! Why'd you do that? They can describe you!'

'We'd already been seen, remember?' Raphael kept his voice low. 'There was nothing to be gained by being anymore. thorough.'

It was a logical explanation, and one that he hadn't needed to give. He owed explanations to his handler only. The truth was he needed to hear himself say the words, to see if they helped disguise the fact that he had been unable to kill another human being with Cat watching. Just injuring them had shocked her to her core. The last thing he had wanted was to increase her level of trauma even further.

'Yeah, I see. I'm sure you're right.' The man looked pointedly at his empty glass.

Raphael slid a twenty pound note across the table. 'Buy yourself a drink.'

'Don't mind if I do. Do you want anything?'

'No. I've got everything I need.'

The man eased out from behind the table and made his way to the bar. When he returned with his beer, Raphael Ward had gone.

He took the long route back to the hotel, walking up Bayswater Road and turning right into Queensway before eventually threading his way back through a series of less busy streets. There was no sign that he was being followed. Despite that, he sat in the hotel reception for fifteen minutes before going up to the room.

Cat was laying on one of the beds. She sat up as he entered. 'You're back quicker than I expected,' she said. 'I was trying to sleep.' She ran a hand through her hair.

'That was a good idea. We don't perform well, and we can't make good decisions if our brain is tired.'

'And how is your brain right now?'

'Doing its job.'

'Which is?'

'Double-checking that my gut instinct about what to do next is right.'

'That sounds the wrong way round. Shouldn't you work out your plan logically and deliberately and then check how you feel about it?'

He shook his head. 'People don't function like that. Most of us like to believe we're rational, logical beings first and foremost, but that's not how we are wired. The truth is we feel emotions first and logical thinking is secondary. That's why you're feeling how you are. If you could just think your way into behaving differently you'd do it. Only the conscious mind doesn't possess such authority. Our sub-conscious and emotions dominate. Once we understand and accept that, it becomes much easier to manage ourselves.'

'So you're a neuroscientist as well as a spy and a black belt?'

'I'm actually none of those things,' Raphael checked his watch. 'But I have decided that my gut instinct is right.'

'And what does that mean exactly?'

'It means we're going to do what no one would expect us to – we're going to attack.'

A part of him shuddered because he knew what that meant. He prayed he could see it through.

14

The bar was decorated predominantly in black and gold with occasional splashes of vibrant red. Eddie Wynn had chosen the colour scheme himself. He hadn't asked the highly experienced, very expensive interior designer he had employed for any advice. Eddie didn't work that way. He told people what he wanted. They made sure it happened, pure and simple.

Eddie paused as he picked up his mobile phone from the bar top and reflected briefly.

Simple.

Not pure.

Nothing about him could be called pure. Not now. Not ever. Unless you regarded always getting your own way as a form of purity.

Eddie shrugged.

He wasn't employed for his abilities as a philosopher. He returned his attention to the phone and made his call. It was answered almost immediately.

'Y-Yes?'

Eddie smiled at the fear in the other man's voice. 'Is everything on schedule?'

'Y-Yes. Absolutely.'

'Are you sure?'

'Of course. I wouldn't lie to you.'

'Wouldn't you?'

'N-No.'

'When we agreed our deal there was no sign of a stammer in your voice.'

The man chose not to reply.

Eddie waited for several seconds, then turned up the pressure. 'So there hasn't been a delay in the transportation process?' He felt rather than heard the other man swallow as his adrenalin increased. 'You see the rumour is, there was a breakdown in Europe.' Eddie slowed his delivery. 'The rumour is you've lost control.'

'That's not true!'

'Really?'

'Everything will be with you as agreed. I give you my word!'

'Excellent. Your word is important to me. And you know what it means when something is important to me.'

'I do.'

'Good.'

Eddie glanced up as the door opened. A blonde walked in. She was wearing tight fitting blue Levi jeans and a brown leather bomber jacket. Eddie didn't recognise her, and he would definitely have remembered if he had seen her before.

She stopped only five feet away from him, placed both of her palms on the bar, smiled at Mikey the bartender and ordered a vodka and tonic with lots of ice.

It was the ice that did it for Eddie, that and the shape of her ass in the tight jeans. He ended his phone call without saying another word. He didn't need to. The point had been made. The threat was clear. And she was close enough to smell her perfume. He put his phone back on the bar top in a way that was guaranteed to make her look.

She did.

'The first drink's on the house,' he said.

She considered obviously and deliberately. 'Because I'm a woman?'

'Because you're the first guest of the day,' he said, 'and because I'm the boss so I can do what I like.'

'In that case I'll make it a double vodka.'

He nodded at Mikey without taking his eyes off her. 'I like women – guests – who are forceful.'

'Then we'll get along just fine,' she said.

He knew then he would fuck her so hard she cried. 'My name's Eddie.'

He reached forwards with an outstretched hand. She took it. He squeezed hard. She did her best to match it. He liked the way the pain brought anger to her eyes.

'I'm Patricia,' she said. 'People call me Pat.'

He let go of her hand. 'What brings you in here so early?' he asked.

'I like dark places,' she said. She took a step closer as she spoke. Mikey placed her drink between them. She put her hand around the glass but didn't pick it up. Her nails were manicured. They were painted vibrant red. Eddie couldn't help but imagine fucking her over the dining room table in his flat, with his secret cameras recording it all.

'Is there anything else I should know about you?' He asked.

'You should know I'm a free spirit,' she said.

'Free enough to do what?'

'Anything I fucking like.'

'Talk's cheap,' he said.

'I'm not cheap,' she smiled. 'I'm free.'

She raised her glass in a silent toast. He put his hand on hers and stopped her from drinking.

'I have much better vodka in my flat,' he said. 'If you want to drink more freely.'

'Sounds ideal.' She turned her back to the bar. 'Let's go.'

15

He lived in a two-bedroomed flat on King Street. It was just a few minutes' walk from the bar. He steered her with his left hand on the small of her back. Occasionally he tightened his grip, squeezing her flesh. She made no attempt to stop him.

'We're here,' he said suddenly, tapping her bottom as he stopped by his building. 'Let's get in.'

He made sure she walked up the stairs in front of him.

He was hard long before they reached the top.

There were two locks to his front door. He smiled at her as he unlocked them, his mind racing. He had already decided he would use the film of them fucking to gain control of her. She would do what he wanted. In return, he would keep the film private.

Pure and simple.

Well...

The man wearing a black balaclava seemed to appear out of nowhere. Eddie tried to respond, but he had no chance. The man's right hand chopped hard into Eddie's carotid artery. He lost consciousness instantly.

Raphael caught the body before it hit the floor. Cat pushed the door open.

'Inside. Quickly!' Raphael held the body as Cat entered the flat. He dragged Eddie in after her. She locked the door behind them. Raphael pulled Eddie into the large living room and tied him to a chair. He removed Eddie's mobile phone and put it in his own pocket.

'I'm going to wake him up now,' he said. 'Say and do nothing until this is over. This is the crucial engagement. If this doesn't end how we need it to, if we don't get the information we need, our mission is over. Do you understand?'

She nodded.

'Good. Stand over there, behind him, next to the table.'

Cat did.

Raphael went into the kitchen and returned with a glass of water. He threw it into Eddie's face. The gangster came to with an immediate threat.

'I'll have you fucking killed for this!'

Raphael slapped him hard across his face. 'You have no power here,' he said. 'In fact, if you want to survive you need to do precisely as I say. If you don't, you will die.'

Eddie strained against his bonds. 'Do you know who I am?' He roared.

'You're my prisoner,' Raphael said calmly. 'And I will be your executioner if you don't submit fully.'

'I don't submit to anyone!' Eddie tried to force himself upright.

Raphael punched him in his solar plexus. The blow took his breath away. 'Your life means nothing to me,' Raphael said. 'You will live to see tomorrow only if you answer my questions. Is that clear?'

Eddie glared. Cat paled.

'Before we go any further,' Raphael said, 'you have to

understand that I know everything there is to know about you. That's why I don't care whether you live or die.'

Eddie had nearly recovered from the blow. His anger was returning. It was mixed with an obvious curiosity.

'I doubt you know half the truth,' he snarled.

'If you want to talk about halves, I know your tattoo is only half-finished.' Raphael smirked. 'What use is half a Samurai? The answer is, no use at all. Although, I guess at least it symbolises you – only half the man you think you are.'

Raphael punched him in the plexus a second time. Eddie's eyes squeezed shut in pain. Cat squealed and turned away. Raphael ignored them both.

He waited until Eddie finally opened his eyes and said, 'If you need me to prove how well I know you, I will tell you everything, one fact after another. And for every fact I have to tell you I will hit you once. Not always in your plexus, that would get boring very quickly. So I'll introduce an element of surprise, just to add a little entertainment to the process. What do you say?'

'I'm going to kill you!'

Raphael laughed. 'You're not. I can assure you of that. But there's the problem, you see? I've only hit you in the same place twice and you're adjusting to it already. That's how adaptive human beings are. So...'

Raphael drove his right elbow down into Eddie's left thigh. The gangster screamed. Cat couldn't keep quiet any longer.

'You've got to stop this!' She yelled.

Raphael barely glanced at her. 'Don't ever tell me how to do my job.' He kept his voice hard and low. 'And don't ever forget why you're here.'

He looked down at Eddie. 'Don't forget why you're here either. Now, are you going to start answering my questions or do we have to keep playing games?'

Eddie licked his lips. He stretched back in the chair. 'You can't escape the pain,' Raphael said. 'At least not like that.' He raised his right elbow suddenly. Eddie flinched. 'Your brain and body are telling you what to do,' Raphael continued. 'If you don't want to listen to me, listen to them. After all, their only concern is your survival. Mine isn't.'

Eddie nodded slowly.

'Good decision. Let's begin.' Raphael stepped back half a pace. 'For all the power you've convinced others you have, I know you're just a link in the chain. I'm interested only in the final link – Sir Desmond Swann. First of all, I want to know who the links in the chain are between you and him. Tell me.' Raphael stepped forward again.

'There's only one,' Eddie spoke quickly. 'But I don't know who it is. It's always a discreet connection. That's what keeps the chain safe.'

'Not true. And I'll tell you why. If you're that close to the top – and I accept you are – you're part of an elite group, and members of elite groups know each other. If they're managed well they stay together, and that's what makes the rest of the chain feel isolated, scared and ambitious in equal measure. Plus, your breathing changed and you spoke too quickly when you said you didn't know who he is. So I know you do.' Raphael paused briefly. 'And the fact that you accept my reference to *him* means it's a man. Which again is no surprise. So tell me his name. If you don't, this time I will break something.' Raphael tapped Eddie's wrist.

Eddie shook his head. 'I can't,' he mumbled. 'I can't tell you.' He tensed as he spoke.

Raphael squatted down in front of him. He placed his right palm over Eddie's left hand. 'Fingers first then wrist then, if necessary, I'll work my way up. Are you sure it's worth it?'

Eddie looked away. He tried to clench his fist, but Raphael

already had control of his middle finger. He straightened it until the fingertip was pointing at the ceiling, then he slowly increased the pressure on the first joint.

'Are you sure it's worth it?' He repeated.

Eddie bit his lower lip. Raphael bent the finger back, close to breaking point. Eddie grimaced. Raphael released his grip suddenly and straightened.

'Sometimes people give away the answer by what they don't say, rather than by what they do,' he said. 'You're not the sort of man who would voluntarily take pain just to protect a colleague. Yet you were preparing yourself for the worst. That can only mean one thing. The man you're protecting is your brother, Mack. I know he's the head of Swann's security. I didn't know to what extent – if any – he was involved in all the bad stuff. Now I do. Thanks to you.'

Eddie spat at Raphael. 'You're a fucking dead man walking!'

'Let's not go back to that, eh? It only caused you grief before.' Raphael checked his watch. 'Time is a friend to neither of us right now, so let's move on to my second question. I'm sure you'll be pleased to know it's my final one. How many safes are there in Swann's penthouse?'

'How the fuck should I know?'

'Because you're the man whose job it is to keep the place secure. Mack might have responsibility for keeping all operations running well and I guess he's tasked with making sure everything looks legit, but you're the man on the ground in London. So how many safes are there?'

Raphael flexed the gloved fingers of his right hand.

'Two,' Eddie looked down as he spoke. 'There's one in the walk-in wardrobe of the master bedroom and another behind one of the paintings in the entrance hall. I don't know any more than that.'

'You've never seen them?'

'No.'

'Or opened them?'

'Of course not! Nobody goes near them apart from the man himself. Mack is the only other person who even knows they exist.'

'I believe you.' Raphael smiled. 'Just one more thing before we go—'

'You said there only two questions!'

'Changed my mind.' Raphael slapped Eddie's left shoulder. The other man flinched instinctively. 'And this really is the last question. How many men have you tasked with watching the place since we visited? Eh?' A second slap, harder this time.

'There's a couple out front. That's all. The main man doesn't like anything to be too obvious.'

'You mean he doesn't like you and your people to be too obvious. He isn't shy about showing off his wealth and his other connections, is he?'

Eddie's face coloured. 'We get looked after well enough.'

'I'm sure you do, up to a point.' Raphael signalled to Cat. 'We're going now. You need to keep still and silent. If I hear another word come out of your mouth I will damage you.' He locked eyes with his prisoner, maintaining his gaze until the other man admitted defeat and looked down again. 'Good.'

Raphael turned and walked out of the flat. Cat followed a pace behind. He could feel the emotions threatening to overwhelm her. He checked his own heartbeat. It was steady at forty-five beats per minute.

16

Cat didn't speak until they were back on the street and walking away from the flat.

'You didn't ask him!' She hissed. 'You tortured him and you enjoyed it, and you didn't ask him about the most important thing!'

'That wasn't torture, it was persuasion based on believable threat. And I asked him everything I needed to.'

'What about my brother?' Cat grabbed him by his upper arm and brought him to a standstill. 'You didn't find out anything about what happened and who was involved. We don't know any more now than we did before!'

'Yes, we do.' Raphael removed her hand gently but firmly. 'We know that either Eddie or his brother Mack ordered the killing. My guess is that Eddie couldn't have done it without his brother's permission. Killing a policeman is as risky as it gets, so it would have needed the highest level of approval. The people who carried it out would have been far more skilled than the two we met at the penthouse. They would most probably have been specialists available for hire. The odds are we'll never discover their identities, but in one sense that doesn't matter.

The men who were ultimately responsible for Peter's murder are the brothers Grimm and their wealthy boss.'

'Then why have we just left Eddie behind? Why didn't you arrest him, or call someone else to come and arrest him, or do whatever it is you do?'

'Timing is everything and that's not my immediate purpose,' Raphael said. 'Besides, what provable crime would we have charged him with? And what do you think his lawyer would have said about the nature of my persuasion?' Raphael began walking again. Cat kept by his shoulder. 'We can't afford to win a battle and then lose the war. We have to be patient, strategic. You won't ever get another chance, so you can't afford to let your desire for victory rush you into defeat.'

'Watching you hit him was horrible,' she said. 'It was even worse than when you beat the men in the penthouse.'

'It was the only way to make him talk – it was certainly the only way in the timeframe we'd got.'

'What you did was illegal, though. How do you justify that?'

'To whom?'

'To yourself, to your bosses.'

I keep a prayer in my heart and I bear the weight of my sins on my shoulders.

'My bosses don't ask. They judge me only on my results.'

'So what makes you better than the so-called bad guys?'

'I didn't kill your brother.'

Raphael crossed the road briskly. As they passed the entrance to the Ritz he gestured ahead and said, 'You need to take the Tube back to Lancaster Gate. Go straight into our room and wait for me there. I will be a few hours behind you.'

'Where are you going?'

It was his turn to stop. 'There are a couple of things I have to do. They are things you don't need to know about.'

'You mean they're illegal?'

'I mean it's best for both of us if you don't know what they are.'

She shook her head angrily. 'Everything we do is one way! I've told you everything I know, and you keep secrets. You make the decisions and I follow along. You expect me to trust you and yet you're doing more and more things that make me wonder just who the hell you really are!'

'I keep secrets in order to keep you safe. I make the decisions because I'm the expert here. Everything I do is intended to protect those things I care about, to make the world a more peaceful place. Please go back to the hotel.'

Cat considered. Raphael saw her think of another question and decide against asking it. 'I don't want to get used to the violence,' she said finally.

'I understand that. I wouldn't want you to.'

A large group of Japanese tourists engulfed them. Some stopped to take photos of the famous hotel. He waited until they had moved on.

'I'll be back as soon as I can.'

She hesitated, looking at the hotel entrance rather than at him. 'Take care,' she said, before setting off to the Tube.

17

The text telling the two men to stand down and take the rest of the day off came from Eddie's mobile phone. It was written in his usual abrupt manner. It demanded an immediate acknowledgement and it didn't invite questions. The unusual thing was the command itself. Eddie never changed his mind once he had given an instruction, and the instruction to watch the penthouse until they were replaced at midnight had been explicit.

The two men wanted to discuss the best thing to do, but neither wanted to be the first to question what they had just read. Eddie didn't take kindly to hesitation or requests for clarification. So the two men hid their surprise, made up stories about how they would spend the rest of their day and left the penthouse unguarded.

Raphael watched them go from his position outside the Coach and Horses pub. When he was certain that neither man was going to return he made his move. Five minutes later he was in the penthouse. Sixty-five minutes later he had opened both safes and been through their contents. He had found a variety of legal documents, some compromising photos of a prominent politician, a very expensive 1950's watch and an envelope containing twenty thousand pounds in fifty pound notes. The *SS* was not there.

Raphael sighed. He had prayed for the mission to end today, more for Cat's sake than his own. He wanted her to get out of this world as quickly as possible. He wanted her to go home with a sense of victory, feeling she had achieved justice for her brother.

If the *SS* had been present Raphael knew precisely the story he would have told Cat to convince her that they – she – had been successful. It was a story he had worked out earlier that day, a series of lies tied together with sufficient truth to make it strong enough to hold on to.

Only now it was irrelevant. There was no need to lie. Not yet, anyway. Now there was one remaining task before turning his attention to Swann's Berkshire mansion. It was the task he had been trying not to think about, the one he had hidden gratefully behind the penthouse search.

Raphael checked that he was leaving behind no signs of his presence and then left the building. He walked the route to his next destination oblivious to the people around him. His thoughts stalled. His mind felt as if it was frozen. His remaining sense of self recognised this as a necessary protective mechanism.

Thoughts – if there had been any – would have urged him to walk in a different direction, to return to the hotel and Cat. Thoughts would have challenged him in ways that might have been too difficult to bear. Thoughts might have turned into questions he didn't want to answer.

So Raphael kept walking, aware vaguely that the promise he had made to his handler was more important than anything else.

A drunk bumped into him, cursing and staggering on his

way without a backwards glance. Raphael's body automatically twisted away from the contact. His mind sprang back to life.

One for the road...

Perhaps one day he would take a journey knowing it would end in his death. Until then he was the executioner, the man who marked the end of the road for others.

Raphael quickened his pace. He had been taught that if he couldn't walk away from an issue it was better to walk forwards quickly, and that if he couldn't avoid a problem it was better to address it immediately. He reached his destination in a matter of minutes. Eddie was still tied in the chair, but he had managed to move it towards the door. His eyes widened when he saw Raphael.

'It's you, isn't it? You're the man in the balaclava, you're still wearing the same clothes.'

Raphael didn't reply. Instead he made a quick check of the other rooms, ensuring no one else was present.

'Wh-What have you come back for? I told you everything I knew.' Eddie spoke quickly, his voice raising. 'There's nothing here for you.'

Raphael returned to face Eddie. 'I'm afraid there is,' he said softly.

'No, you've got it wrong! I can't do anymore for you, and no one's gonna start looking for me until tomorrow. You've got plenty of time to get away!'

'You saw her,' Raphael said. 'That means sooner or later you will track her down. Then, whenever you've done what you want to with her, you will kill her – or have her killed, just as you did her brother.'

'What? Who are you talking about?' Eddie shook his head wildly, fear playing across his face.

'Her brother was an undercover policeman. He was interested in Swann's illegal arms deals. Either you or Mack had him tortured and killed, and then made a point of leaving his body in the trash.'

'No! No! You've got this all wrong! I didn't do that!'

'You did. I just saw it in your face – the recognition when I described what happened to him. At first you didn't know who I was talking about, but you'd remembered clearly by the time I mentioned how the body was left,' Raphael looked over Eddie's shoulders. 'Anyway, that's in the past. I can't save him, but I can save her. And I have to.'

He reached inside his jacket and removed the knife from the shoulder sheath.

Eddie thrashed against his bonds. 'No! Please! I can get you anything you want! Please—'

As the gangster pleaded for his life, Raphael sought to calm his mind. He tried to access the state that had, until recently, been so familiar to him. He reminded himself why the man needed to die, how Cat's immediate safety depended upon it. Yet, despite his best efforts, the knife felt heavy in his hand.

Raphael closed his eyes, placed the blade against his chest, and prayed for the strength to do what was right.

For the first time ever, the words rang hollow.

18

Cat had showered and changed by the time he returned to the hotel.

'I bought some new clothes on my way back,' she said. 'I guessed you'd have been unhappy if I'd nipped home to get stuff.'

'You're right. Good thinking.'

'So, how did everything go?'

'It confirmed there is nothing more that can be done in London.'

'Where do we go next?'

'I don't think *we* should go anywhere.'

'No! No!' Cat raised her right hand, like a police officer bringing traffic to a halt. 'We've got a deal. I stay with you until you've accomplished your mission and I've got concrete evidence against Swann and his henchmen for the murder of Peter. You make the decisions and I follow your lead. That's the deal. There's no going back on that. We didn't agree to do this together only in London. We didn't put a geographical or time limit on this, so don't try to create one now!'

'I got evidence whilst I was out that proved I was right about

Peter's death. Eddie and Mack were responsible. There is no doubt.'

'What is it? Where is it?'

'It was what I was told, it wasn't something I could bring back with me.'

'Who told you?'

'It doesn't matter.'

'Of course it matters! You identify the person – or people – to the police, they question them and, at the very least, a whole new area of investigation opens up!'

'The people we are dealing with don't confess to the police just because they're brought in for questioning. You should have worked that out already.'

'Then why don't you capture them and get them to tell you? You can record what they say, make them name everyone involved.'

Raphael gave her a second to realise what she had just said.

'Oh, dear God...' Cat sat down. 'What am I thinking?'

'You're feeling, not thinking. That's how we function, remember?'

She nodded. 'I have to see this through with you. It's the only way I'm going to keep – or regain – my sanity.'

'You haven't lost your sanity and I don't want you to be at risk of losing anything else. They know about us. They'll be on the lookout. It's going to be even more difficult from now on.'

'I don't care. Besides, now that Eddie knows me, I'm a target. Aren't I? I'm not stupid. I have worked it out. I'm safer with you than if I go home or try to hide somewhere on my own. You know that's right.'

'No, I don't. In fact, I know you're wrong. If I do my job correctly you'll only have to keep yourself safe for a couple of days, and during that time they'll be too busy dealing with me to come looking for you.'

'And what if you don't do your job correctly, what if you fail? Then I'll be at their mercy, won't I?'

'I don't fail.'

Cat waved her hand dismissively. 'Whilst I'm nowhere near as skilled as you at this kind of work, I am just as committed. I'm just as willing to risk and sacrifice. Please don't think that because I'm a woman I'm weak. History is filled with women who have committed to a cause and seen it through!'

'But this doesn't have to be your challenge, and besides, you've done enough already.'

'No, I haven't. I know the violence sickens me, and to be honest, I'm terrified about what else you might do, but I have to get to the end of this. Just like you do.'

'Imagine a situation,' he said, 'in which I'm seconds away from being killed by one of Swann's men. You have a loaded gun in your hand and your choice is simple – kill the man and save my life or let him live and watch me die. What would you do?'

'That's not fair,' she said. 'Why couldn't I just hit him over the head with the gun?'

'So you would be willing to cause him brain damage in order to save me?'

She frowned.

'What would you have done in order to save Peter?' He asked.

Her eyes flooded. 'Anything,' she whispered.

'Then be willing to do anything now,' he said.

Cat wiped the tears away. 'Are we going to finish this together?'

He nodded slowly. 'Yes.'

'So, back to my first question – where are we going?'

'I'll tell you tomorrow morning when we leave here. Right now I have to go back out and meet with my contact. I need some more information so that I can plan fully.' It was a lie and he told it easily. It was the least of his sins. 'This is the last time I'm going to ask you to stay here and wait for me. I promise.'

'Ok.'

Raphael smiled reassuringly and made a point of closing the door gently behind him. He waved a soft, unseen farewell as he strode along the corridor.

He had no intention of ever seeing her again.

PART II

THE MAN WITH EVERYTHING...

19

Sir Desmond Swann stood on the raised patio at the rear of his seven bedroomed Berkshire mansion and looked out across the fields that surrounded his extensive grounds. He gloried in the fact that he owned all of the land for as far as he could see. He had made sure that everyone knew. And that everyone knew to keep well away.

Swann sipped his coffee and breathed in the clear Autumn air. It had long been his opinion that land was the most significant possession a man could own. Anything else was inevitably the work of other men. But land was God's creation. When you owned land you had control of God's handiwork. It became subject to your will, not God's. It reflected a level of power few could even imagine.

'Excuse me, sir?'

Swann turned. Rupert, the butler, was standing in the open kitchen doorway.

'What is it?'

'Mr Wynn is here. He says there's a matter he needs to share with you.'

'You put him in my study?'

'As always, sir.'

'Good. Tell him I'll be there shortly.'

'Very well, sir.'

Swann looked back at his grounds and the fields beyond. A low, simple wooden fence marked the boundary of his property. Nothing more. He didn't need any more security than that. There were always men on site – men chosen personally by Wynn – and besides, everyone knew who he was. No one was stupid enough to trespass, let alone attempt a more serious invasion. Reputation was the best possible security system and his reputation was well established.

Swann poured his remaining coffee onto the patio and went inside to hear Wynn's news. The younger man rose to his feet as Swann entered the room. There was anger in his eyes and a tension in his body.

'Mack,' Swann crossed to the burgundy leather chair behind his desk. 'I see from your demeanour that something very serious has happened. What is it?'

'Eddie's dead. Murdered. Assassinated in his flat,' Mack hissed the words out. 'Someone killed my brother in his own fucking flat!'

'I am deeply sorry.' Swann sat. 'Do we have any insights yet into who and why?'

'We have some footage from the secret cameras Eddie used to film himself fucking women—'

'I didn't know of those.'

'I didn't think it was a detail you needed to be informed of. Anyway, the footage doesn't show everything that happened because Eddie was barely in the camera's view. We do know that a blond woman and a guy in a black balaclava were present. Eddie hooked up with the blond at the bar. Mikey the barman said she made it clear she was up for it. From what we can see, she just stood back, watching. Actually it looks like she was struggling to cope with what was happening. It was obviously the guy who did the work. He knocked Eddie around enough to make him answer his questions—'

'What did he want to know?'

'About your safes in the penthouse. He came back later, after the first visit, and asked about the death of that undercover cop we dealt with. That's when he must have killed him,' Mack blanched. 'We can't see anything on this film, because Eddie had shifted himself across the floor, but it's got to have been this same guy. It was a professional job, a single stab wound to the heart. The weird thing is, sounds like the guy says a prayer or something before leaving.'

'A prayer?'

'We can't be sure. His voice was really low, but that's what it sounds like. You know, like a priest at a funeral.'

Swann tapped his fingers on the desktop. 'A killer priest,' he mused. 'Well spotted. Can we assume that this is the man who beat up Eddie's boys so easily?'

'Yes.'

'And he asked about my safes and the dead policeman?'

'Yes.'

'And nothing else?'

'As far as we can tell.'

'Hmm. For reasons I'm not going to explain, I'm certain this is not primarily an act of revenge. This isn't just about someone paying Eddie back for the death of that undercover policeman. There is something far greater at play here. Which is why I'm quite surprised by this turn of events.' Swann was thoughtful for a moment. 'You've checked the penthouse again I take it?'

'Yes.'

'Has anything been taken?'

'No.'

'And the safes?'

'Unopened, still secure. But...'

'But what?'

'The men Eddie had watching the place were told to stand down. They believed the message came from Eddie, so they did.'

'So my home was left unprotected even though there was an identified threat?' Swann stiffened.

'Yes, sir.'

'Please ensure that in future we don't employ men who can be tricked by a text message.'

'Yes, sir.'

'And do ensure those men are dismissed today.'

'I will.'

Swann nodded. 'Ensure too that they depart with a leaving present they will never forget.'

'Sir.'

'Right. Moving on, I think we can assume that our prayerful killer tricked Eddie's men so that he could return to the penthouse, and that he is so good he was able to search everywhere thoroughly, including the safes, and leave no evidence of his visit. I am confident that we are dealing with a most highly trained professional.'

Mack knew better than to speak. He stood very still.

'My greatest concern in this regard is the timing of it all. Given that we are less than forty-eight hours away from what will undoubtedly be the most spectacular auction in history, you will treat this man's presence as an imminent and most serious threat.'

'But if he's targeting the auction, and if he's so skilled, why would he bring himself to our attention? Why would he even bother with Eddie?'

'Every search has to start somewhere, every mission has a first step.' Swann sat back in his chair. 'However, rather than wonder about what he has done already, we need to determine what he is about to do.'

'I agree, but he could be targeting any aspect of our – your – operations. Why are you so sure it's the auction?'

'I've already told you!' Swann snapped. 'Weren't you listening? I don't believe in coincidences! I am about to auction the most prized religious object known to man and a professional killer, who feels the need to pray over his victims, targets us suddenly. What do you think the odds are of that happening by accident?'

'Billions to one.' Mack's voice trailed off as his mind raced with the security implications. 'You can rest assured that one man won't disrupt your plans, especially now that we are on to him.'

'Please don't underestimate the threat he poses.' Swann was stern. 'Please regard him as at least as proficient as yourself.'

Mack frowned. 'With all due respect, sir, that's impossible. You know my background, that's why you employed me in the first place. There is nothing comparable.'

'When we believe something is impossible, we create an opening for defeat,' Swann said. 'Remember that.'

'I will.' Mack paused briefly. 'Do you want him killed on sight?'

'If there's no alternative. Ideally, though, I'd like to meet him and share a few things before you do your worst. Either way, he needs to disappear completely.'

'Understood.'

'Get to it then.'

'Sir.' Mack reached the door in four, quick strides. 'And Mack?'

He turned abruptly. 'Sir?'

'I'll pay for your brother's funeral. We'll make sure it's a good one.'

'Thank you, sir.'

Swann nodded. When the door closed, he reached down and removed a well-worn book from a desk drawer. He placed it in front of him, his right hand resting briefly on the cover. It was an original 1611 version of the King James Bible. Swann looked down at it. He reminded himself that, for all its age and value, it had been written by men. He thought of his land. He nodded to himself and made a phone call.

20

The bald, overweight man, with flecks of alcohol-induced violet in his cheeks and emotionless eyes, finished his telephone conversation without once acknowledging the messenger who had just entered his office. Instead he kept his back to him and stared out of the large, double-glazed window at the familiar view.

He looked at the large plaza with its colonnades, obelisk and paving marked with radiating lines, in the same way a gallery owner looked at a great painting hanging on one of their walls. He appreciated it not just for its beauty, but also for its ability to draw people in. He enjoyed being able to watch the crowds without ever being seen. He could sense their neediness. He knew how to feed it.

When he ended the call, he spoke without turning around.

'I trust you have information for me that is fully up to date?'

'I do.'

'Speak.'

'I have been informed that our operative—'

'My operative.'

'Yes. Yes, of course. My apologies. Your operative is doing

precisely as expected in almost all respects. He has finished his work in the capital and is now closing in on the primary target, Sir Desmond Swann. That gentleman, for his own part, is aware of the threat but is planning to go ahead as scheduled. He is trusting, we presume, that his security will prove too much for one man.'

'How interesting that we so easily forget the power that one man can wield. How fascinating that this is most easily forgotten by men who are themselves powerful.' The bald man smiled. 'You said he was doing well in almost all respects?'

'Yes.'

'Then in what respect is he not doing well?'

'He, er, he is not working alone.'

The bald man spun round. 'What?'

'He... he has a woman with him. It seems that she crossed his path at the beginning of his mission.'

'And?'

'He has had several opportunities to terminate their relationship efficiently but has chosen not to.'

'What has he revealed to her?'

'Nothing as far as we can tell.'

'But you cannot be sure?'

'Not at this moment. It is, of course, expected that he will reveal nothing, given his training.'

'It is expected that he work alone!' The bald man roared. 'It is expected that he does only what he is ordered to! And I do not need your opinions – I expect only facts!'

'Of course. I'm sorry.' The messenger bowed. 'The latest information I have is that he is now travelling alone, that he has left her behind.'

'And she is where?'

'I don't know.'

'Find out. I want to know where she is, who she is and to whom she is connected. Make it a priority.'

'I will.'

'Start now.'

The messenger bowed again and backed out of the room.

The bald man turned back to face the window and the familiar view. Below him people crossed the plaza, some pointed at architecture, some stopped to take photos. The bald man smiled at their devotion and naivety. He thanked God for the power of belief.

21

The car provided for him was a dark blue Volvo v70. It was parked in an underground car park on Queensway, just a short walk from the Lancaster Gate hotel. The keys were hidden on top of the driver's front wheel. The petrol tank was full.

Raphael had memorised the route. He was avoiding the motorways and using, instead, the A40 followed by a mixture of A and B roads. It was a journey of less than fifty miles.

It took him just over an hour.

Cookham is a small village on the river Thames. Its inhabitants are mostly wealthy; many of them make the daily commute into the capital. Swann's home was situated on the outskirts of the village.

Raphael knew where he could hide the car. He knew an excellent vantage point from where he could study the comings and goings at the mansion. He had maps of the surrounding land and plans of the mansion and all the associated buildings.

Raphael eased the Volvo off the road and parked it out of sight behind a long, narrow barn on land that was owned by a wealthy friend of the Church. He turned off the engine and sat, unmoving, for several minutes.

The auction hadn't taken place yet. The *SS* hadn't been sold. He was sure of that. In London his presence had become obvious. Here he had to be covert. His activities in the capital would have put Swann on the alert, security would have been increased and teams would have been tasked with tracking him down.

And finding Cat, too.

He had been thinking about that a great deal since he had cast her adrift without warning. The odds were that she had found the note he had left in the bathroom. In it, he apologised and told her to find a new place in which she could lay low for the next few days. He hoped she had acted on his advice. He prayed she went somewhere that was in no way connected to her usual routines.

There was no doubt that by going after Swann, Cat had put her own life at risk. It was also true that by helping her he had increased that risk, and put his own mission in jeopardy, too. He knew his handler would find that unforgivable. He couldn't help but wonder if Pietro, by the end of his life, would have had a very different perspective.

The day before he died, Pietro had summoned him and said, 'Weakness teaches much that strength cannot. Now, because my illness has forced me into ever-greater periods of stillness, I have a lesson or you. I fear it will be one of my last. It is simply this, the greatest mission is the mission of the heart.'

That was why he had let Cat live, why he had only injured the two men in the penthouse, why the need to kill Eddie had been so challenging. Taking another human life no longer felt like a mission of the heart. In fact, it felt like the opposite.

Raphael reviewed his journey from London.

He had chosen the route because lesser-used roads made it far more difficult for someone to tail you without being spotted. At times he had driven slowly, forcing cars to overtake him. At other times he had deliberately broken the speed limit, keen to study any car that followed his lead. He had stopped at two garages, buying water at one and chocolate at the other. Both times he had made a mental note of the first three cars that drove past; he hadn't seen them again. Yet, despite all of his precautions, he still had the feeling that he had been followed.

His logical mind told him it wasn't possible. His gut screamed out a different message. Raphael reviewed the journey one final time. Nothing stood out. No car, or series of cars, no face behind a windscreen. No sign of anything out of the ordinary. So why was his gut so sure? What had his subconscious noticed that it wasn't sharing? Raphael ran both hands around the circle of the steering wheel. At times like this, gut instinct had to be allowed to triumph over logic. The conscious mind had to be subdued and brought under control, just as a dog had to be trained to return to heel. This was part of the discipline he had learnt both as a monk and as a member of the Mystiko Kataskopos. It meant that he had to assume he had been followed, that he was being watched. That meant, in all likelihood, someone was sharing information with Swann and his people.

But who?

Raphael considered. Swann's men had been onto him almost from the very beginning. Originally he had thought that was because of Cat's inability to remain unnoticed. Now, though, he had to explore other options.

He identified three. They were all bad. The second and third were increasingly frightening. The simplest explanation was that the contact he had met in the Swan pub had betrayed him. He had been his only point of contact, he had known of Raphael's presence from the very beginning, he had shared the information about Eddie, and provided the car. True, he had carried out this role for the Church for several years, but that didn't guarantee his fidelity. In Raphael's experience, the easiest individuals to corrupt were those who operated at street-level, who were required at times to blur the edges between one side and another.

Raphael replayed their meeting in his mind. The pointless chatter about the condemned man, the nervous energy and the need for more beer. Irritating perhaps, but actually no different from their first meeting years earlier. There was certainly nothing he had seen to suggest the contact had switched sides.

Which left options two and three.

The second option was that he had misjudged Cat. It led to the inevitable conclusion that when he had first seen her on Hill Street opposite the penthouse, she had been guarding the building, rather than studying it.

The second option turned on the fact that, instead of trying to bring Swann down, Cat was actually working for him. Which meant she was highly skilled, because until now Raphael hadn't even considered that possibility.

If Cat did work for Swann, she would have been told very quickly about Eddie's death, plus she would have known that Raphael was planning to leave London. Whilst he had avoided telling her any great truths about himself and his mission, he had revealed far more than he would have shared willingly with an enemy operative. The bottom line was, if option two was right, Cat knew far more about him and his abilities than he did about her. Raphael shook his head. He didn't want to believe this about her. He didn't want her to be aligned with a man like Swann. Ironically, that meant he wanted her to be a suffering sister, grieving for the loss of a much-loved family member. Yet if she was, that made option three the reality.

Raphael's hands came together in a position of prayer.

They moved of their own volition against his lips.

Option three was the worst of all options. Option three was

that someone senior in the Church, someone who had perhaps even sanctioned his mission, was working secretly with Swann. Someone who claimed to have dedicated their life to the service of God was corrupting their office.

They were using their knowledge and influence to pursue a personal agenda, playing their part in the sale of the Church's most holy object and in the deaths of innocents.

If that was true, who was there left he could trust?

Raphael's hands came apart. His breath had misted the windscreen. He was alone with three options, going from bad to worse. All three threatened the success of his mission; all increased the risks he faced. Two of them forced him to question his abilities as an operative to read people, to make the right decisions and to take the right action. One threatened to tear his worldview apart.

Raphael took the keys out of the ignition and got out of the car. There was nothing more to be gained by reviewing the possibilities. The answer was going to be found by taking action. He put a small bag over his shoulder and jogged towards the vantage point.

The feeling that he was being followed stayed with him.

22

Raphael walked to a wooded area at the top of a small hill. He took a tactical spotting scope from out of the bag and lay down beside a tree. The telescope was the sort used by the world's elite military. It was just over twelve inches long, with a rubber-armoured aluminium body and a water-repellent lens coating. It enabled him to look down into the drive and the courtyard at the front of Swann's mansion and see everything that was happening in complete detail.

Raphael settled in, making himself part of the landscape, as still as the tree he was next to. Now he had to count the men, identify their routines, clarify the levels of security, determine any vulnerability and double-check the entry and exit points. He had to commit it all to memory.

Currently there were four men between the entrance to the grounds and the mansion itself. To the untrained eye, two appeared to be gardeners whilst two were stablehands working in the stables that lined the right side of the drive. Raphael knew better. They all moved like men who were employed because they possessed a very specific skill set. They were all far more alert than normal household staff. They would not be the only ones either. Raphael was sure there would be two teams with up to seven men in each, one team resting whilst the other was active. At any given time one team member would be running a high-tech monitoring system covering every building and all of the land.

Raphael presumed they would be using the perimeter principle. In essence this was a simple model highlighting the number of boundaries, both virtual and physical, that an environment had. Once identified, a security team could then monitor not only each perimeter, but also the transitions and interactions that could occur between them. The goal was to recognise and address a potential threat at the earliest possible perimeter. It was a principle that had changed little from the time the first humans had begun creating secure places in which to live.

Raphael made a series of mental notes about the men and then shifted his focus to the mansion's ground floor windows. He looked from left to right, starting with what he knew to be the entertainment suite and moving across to the first of two lounges, the dining room and the downstairs study. It was there he saw who he was looking for.

Swann.

He was sitting at his desk, reading from a laptop. Next to that was an old, well-worn book that Raphael recognised instantly. It was an original King James Bible.

Raphael gasped. It was the last thing he had expected to see.

The billionaire looked incredibly confident and calm, despite the huge risk he was taking in auctioning the *SS*. Raphael knew there were countless groups and individuals who would go to any lengths to acquire it. By inviting bidders, even though they would have been selected with extreme care, Swann was inviting unwanted attention of the most dangerous kind; hence the need for maximum security and secrecy.

Raphael guessed that Swann had told no one, not even Mack, where he kept the *SS*. It followed, therefore, that only Swann could take him to it. Raphael's plan was to get to him without the security team realising. He would then do whatever it took to make Swann reveal the whereabouts. It was precisely the sort of simple plan that required a high level of expertise if it was to be successful. It was the kind of simplicity Cat had questioned not so long ago.

Raphael felt his mind tug him back to his previous review. If he had time, he would also force Swann to reveal his informant. His handler needed to know their identity. Raphael watched the slim, dark-haired billionaire working behind his desk. He could see him clearly. The long, thin fingers, the narrow nose and golden wire-framed glasses, the signet ring stamped with a family crest on the little finger of his right hand. He looked more like an entitled aristocrat, or a high-level accountant, than one of the most dangerous criminals on the planet.

Raphael wondered if Swann had ever killed anyone himself, or if he had even been present at one of the many executions he had ordered. He guessed that he hadn't done either. Why burden yourself with such activities when you could pay others to do it for you?

Maybe, Raphael mused, by keeping his distance from the violence and death he orchestrated, Swann believed his hands were clean when he touched his Bible?

He glanced at his own hands and Cat's tearful question came back to him.

How does it feel...causing that much harm to another human being?

His answer had been one of the few completely truthful things he had told her.

You can't do it well if you don't really want to...

He was the best operative in the MK because he had trained

more diligently than anyone else. In an organisation based on devotion, he had been desperate to prove himself the most devoted, willing to undertake any training and perform any task, in order to demonstrate his love of God and the Church.

He had done it faultlessly, until this mission. Until something inside him had changed and he had softened his approach.

Now, with the end game closing in, he had to resurrect his old self, the one he had worked so hard to create. The one who never hesitated and who didn't make stupid decisions, the one who was able to wash blood off his hands and then pick up his Bible a second later.

Raphael turned his attention back to the man behind the desk.

'I will do whatever it takes,' he whispered. 'I will force you to tell me the truth, and despite any promises I make, when you have given me everything I need, I will kill you.'

Swann stood up suddenly. Raphael watched him stride across the office and take a book from the bookshelf on the far wall. He looked at a very specific page, wiped some dust off the shelf with his fingertips and replaced the volume.

At that moment a black Range Rover swept into the drive. Raphael trained his scope on it. The windows were blacked out. One of the four men working at the front of the mansion raised a hand in greeting. The car sped past. It came to a halt next to a Green Bentley parked near the stables.

The man in the front passenger seat got out first. Raphael recognised him as Mack. He scanned the grounds automatically, one swift continual turn of the head that missed nothing. Then he nodded at the Range Rover's other occupants.

The rear doors opened. A man Raphael didn't know got out. A blonde woman wearing tight blue jeans followed him.

It was Cat. Raphael tensed when he saw her. She stood with

her head bowed whilst Mack spoke. She nodded twice in response.

Raphael couldn't see her face so he studied her body language, keen to answer the essential question: was Cat there because she worked for Swann or because she was their prisoner?

Mack continued to talk. Cat's chin remained down, low over her throat. Her shoulders were slumped, rounded. Her arms hung, lifeless by her sides. She looked more dispirited and defeated than Raphael had ever seen her.

That didn't necessarily answer the question, though. It was possible she was in trouble with her employer for letting Raphael leave London alone, that by losing contact with him she had failed in her task. It was equally possible, of course, that she had ignored his note and continued in her ill-advised pursuit of Swann. Either possibility would explain her presence and her demeanour.

Raphael eased the tension out of his body and slowed his breathing, just as he would if he was preparing to take a shot at one of the people in his sights. Right now, he needed his mind calm and his senses at their most acute.

What exactly was he looking at?

Before he could reach a conclusion, Mack took a phone out of his pocket and made a call. As he did so he placed his left hand on Cat's shoulder. Raphael saw her flinch.

Two seconds later his burner phone began ringing.

23

Raphael lowered the spotting scope. He hadn't given this number to anyone.

That was the protocol all MK operatives followed. He rolled onto his back and looked up at the golden browns and reds of the tree's foliage. The phone continued to ring. Given that he hadn't shared the number, the obvious conclusion was that someone had taken it. Only one person could have done that.

Raphael turned back to his original position, brought the scope up to his right eye and answered the call. He saw Mack speak a split second before he heard his voice.

'I wondered if you were going to ignore me.'

'I considered it.'

'I've heard that you're not much of a conversationalist.'

'I've heard that you're not much of anything.'

'You heard wrong.' Mack looked up at the hill and woodland where Raphael was hiding. 'I'm more trouble than you can handle. I beat you every day of the week – and that was before you killed my brother.'

'Who says that I did?'

'The security cameras in his flat, the ones you didn't know about.'

'I see.'

'Or rather you didn't see, which is poor for a man in your line of work, wouldn't you say?'

'I'd say it's proof that human beings are fallible, which is why we all lose sooner or later.'

'It's why people like you lose. It's why people like me beat you every day of the week.'

'You sound very sure of yourself.'

'I have every reason to be. Before I took up this role, I'd received the best military training in the world and I'd tested it against people far more dangerous than you.'

'Maybe it's my weakness you should be concerned about, not my strength.'

'Ha! She said at times you talked like a vicar!' Mack took his hand off Cat's shoulder and touched her hair. She pulled away.

'What made her tell you that?'

'Unlike you, I'm a very good conversationalist.'

'Or are you just persuasive?'

'I find the two go hand in hand, although sometimes I do prefer to be simply persuasive. I'm sure you understand what I mean?'

Raphael didn't reply.

'I'll take that as confirmation,' Mack said. He looked back up at the hill. 'I'm guessing you're not too far away?'

'I'm afraid you'll just have to keep guessing.'

Mack laughed. 'I don't need to. One way or another we're going to reel you in, it really doesn't matter where you are.'

'You think I'm hooked, do you?'

'More than you realise.'

Raphael saw a look of confidence playing on the other man's face. Next to him Cat was unmoving.

'There's a world of difference between making a phone call and reeling in a catch,' Raphael said.

'Not on this occasion. Unless you're willing to let someone else suffer on your behalf.' Mack signalled to the man standing behind Cat. He grabbed her arms, pulling them behind her back, pinning them together. Raphael saw, rather than heard, her scream.

Mack said, 'We'll pretend that you can't see me, so I will tell you what's about to happen. I have your friend Catherine Morgan here with me. I know she stood by and watched whilst you tortured my brother. She didn't know, until I told her, that you stabbed him to death. She was shocked when she heard that. She said something about there being a darkness inside you that really scared her. Anyway, that's a side note. Whilst she didn't help you to kill Eddie, she was your original accomplice; you wouldn't have got to him without her help. So I'm going to treat her the way you treated him.'

'She's an innocent in all of this,' Raphael said quickly.

'Is she?'

Raphael closed his eyes briefly. Was she an innocent, or did she carry her own dark secrets and burdens, too? 'If you've seen the footage from Eddie's flat, you know she is,' he said eventually.

'That answer was far too slow coming,' Mack said. 'Either you're not sure or you don't care what happens to her. Regardless, you are forcing me to move proceedings along. As far as I can tell from the footage, you began by punching my brother. I presume that you targeted his solar plexus; it would make sense to create pain and disrupt his breathing at the same time. We both know that gives the brain two major problems to deal with and, thereby, affects the decision-making process.' Mack stopped talking.

Raphael remained silent. Several seconds passed. Mack chuckled. It reminded Raphael of a dog growling.

'I want you to know,' Mack said, 'that I don't have a racist or sexist bone in my body. I hurt everyone equally.' He chuckled again.

Raphael watched him make a point of clenching his right hand and raising the fist in the air. Cat squirmed. Her captor held her tight.

'Solar plexus it is,' Mack said.

'Wait!' Raphael's voice sounded more desperate than he intended. 'She doesn't deserve this!'

Mack lowered his fist. 'So you really do want to save her. Or at least buy her some time. Either way, you are showing weakness – and it certainly isn't one that I need to be concerned about.'

'Unlike you, I'm not in the business of hurting innocent people.'

'Often we don't have a choice. You know that as well as I do.'

'Maybe we let ourselves believe that too easily?'

'Hmm.' Mack nodded thoughtfully. 'It looks like the Boss was right, just as he always is. He said you would put her first. I was sure he was wrong, but he obviously knows you better than I do.'

'He obviously does.' Raphael couldn't help but say the words. The three options he had been evaluating were now down to two. He hadn't told his London contact about Cat and there was no way he could have found out, so option one was off the table. That meant either Cat was working for Swann and what he had been watching for the last few minutes was a charade, or for some reason a senior member of the Church wanted him to fail.

The informant had to be Cat, surely?

Raphael focused the scope solely on her. She was still acting the part perfectly. That made sense. She had been faultless in London. Raphael turned the scope back onto Mack. He was smiling. He waved in Raphael's direction and said something to the man holding Cat's arms. He released her immediately.

At that moment Raphael heard a twig snap. He spun round. Two men were standing eight feet away from him. They were both pointing Glock G19 pistols at his chest. Raphael raised his hands slowly.

Mack's voice sounded on the phone. 'Told you we'd reel you in.'

24

They used handcuffs to fasten his wrists behind his back. Then they searched him swiftly and thoroughly. One removed the knife from its sheath and slid it under the belt in his jeans. The other took his phone. Then they walked him slowly down the hill. They kept several feet behind him, one on his left and one to his right. Apart from giving him the most basic instructions, they didn't speak. They kept their weapons pointing at him throughout.

As they made their way up the drive some of the other men stared at Raphael with interest. He avoided making direct eye contact with any of them. His brain wanted to predict what was about to happen. His feet just wanted to feel the planet. He surrendered to his feet.

The drive led to a large paved area at the front of the house. Six steps brought them up onto a patio. The men directed him into the house through the main doors. Mack was waiting for them in the entrance hall.

He looked Raphael up and down as he stepped forwards. 'Once the Boss has had his conversation with you, you're mine. That's the deal. For some reason Sir Desmond is really interested in you and wants a face-to-face. After that, we're going to have a communication of a very different kind.'

Raphael didn't reply.

Mack punched him hard in his lower abdomen.

Raphael doubled over.

'Normally I don't get emotionally involved,' Mack said. 'I just do what I have to and move on. But you killed my brother. That makes it very personal.'

Raphael forced himself to straighten. Mack punched him again in exactly the same place. Raphael's knees buckled, but he stayed on his feet.

'Unfortunately, I'm not going to have as much time as I'd like with you. There is a rather pressing matter that I have to focus on and that has to take precedent. Still, where time is concerned, I'm a firm believer in the principle of waste-not, want-not.'

A third punch, harder than the previous two, landed in exactly the same place.

Raphael went down onto one knee.

'I guess that's what's called bowing to the inevitable.' Mack glanced at his men. They both smiled. 'To be honest, I expected you to remain standing for longer than that. I'm disappointed.'

Raphael's body wanted to curl into the foetal position. He forced himself upright.

'I only ever bow to the inevitable,' he said, 'and you're not it.'

The fourth blow took all of his strength and self-control away. He collapsed at Mack's feet. The two men stepped forwards and picked him up by his arms.

'Take him downstairs,' Mack ordered. 'Make sure he's secure.'

They half-dragged, half-carried him to a lift. The journey down was swift. The lift door opened, lighting a room that was otherwise pitch black. Raphael kept his eyes closed, letting his body hang between them as they moved him. They kept the handcuffs on and fastened his arms and ankles to a heavy wooden chair. One of them couldn't resist slapping him before they left. The lift door closed. The darkness was complete.

He heard the sound of the lift as it made its way up to ground level. He heard the door open and the men get out. He welcomed that because it meant his breathing had returned to normal and was no longer blocking his senses. He let his mind reach out into the darkness. He knew the impenetrable nature it suggested was a falsehood. He knew the darkness wanted to be silent, but never could be. So he listened into it.

He heard her a split-second before he felt her presence. She was to his left, seated on the far side of the room. He guessed she was tied just as he was. He didn't speak for several minutes, using the time to sense her attitude and intention, keeping his eyes closed, seeking to understand her as if for the first time.

She spoke suddenly, interrupting his exploration. 'Have they hurt you?'

He opened his eyes. The darkness seemed less dense. He saw it shimmer. 'They did,' he said.

'Why— Why do you say it like that?'

'Because it doesn't hurt anymore. My mind and body are used to shedding pain quickly.'

'I'm so sorry for what I've done,' Cat's voice trembled. 'Truly, I am.'

The emotion was believable, as convincing as a great actor inhabiting a role. The fact that she was here now meant there were still things they didn't know, that they thought he was more likely to be tricked rather than beaten into revealing secrets.

'What have you done?' he asked. 'Truthfully?'

'I've done everything wrong. I didn't follow your rules. I didn't take your advice. I ignored your note. I couldn't let go of my desire to catch Swann. Even though my time with you proved that I'm not equipped to do the job, I still thought I knew best. Or, maybe, to be more honest, I was still incapable of thinking clearly. I was being run by my emotions, just as you said I was.'

'So what did you do?'

'I guessed you'd be coming here, after all it's the only other property Swann owns in the UK, so I came too.'

'You got here almost as quickly as I did, and I left first.

How did you manage that?'

'A friend gave me a lift on his motorbike.'

'Did you persuade your friend to simply drop you off and then return to London, no questions asked?'

'Yes.'

'Then your friend lacks any degree of curiosity.'

'My friend is trusting. He was just pleased to help. Don't you have friends like that?'

He ignored the question. He could see her now. Not fully, but enough to decide that his guess was right; she was tied. He was impressed by their thoroughness.

He asked, 'What happened once your friend left?'

'I walked along the high street, hoping that maybe I'd see Swann out and about. I'm not sure what I was planning to do if I did.' She let out a nervous laugh. 'Then I made my way over here. I didn't get very far before the men in the Range Rover grabbed me. It was even more frightening than watching you hurt people.'

'But they didn't harm you?'

'No. I gave them no reason to. I was too scared to try and resist them.'

'That's understandable.' Raphael looked straight ahead, using his peripheral vision to watch her, aware that her eyes were at least as accustomed to the dark as his. 'How did Mack get my phone number?'

'I— I don't know,' she said quickly. 'I guess somebody must have passed it on.'

'The problem is, I hadn't shared the number with anyone else. In fact, the only person I spent any obvious time with in London is you.'

'I didn't do it! I never had access to your phone. And besides, why would I? You were helping me. We are on the same side. The only reason we're both here is because...' Her voice trailed off. He waited and watched in the darkness. 'Oh my God,' her voice dropped to a whisper. 'You think I'm working for them, don't you? You think I'm actually spying on you. That's absolutely...'

'Absolutely what?'

'Insane.' He saw her head turn to face him. 'Whatever your secret reason is for hunting Swann, my reason is greater! My cause – as you would call it – is far stronger and more important than yours! And I'm a Detective Constable. I'm a member of the best police force in the world. So was my brother. We serve people and we follow rules. Unlike you, we are accountable to the public. Unlike you, we don't automatically assume the worst of our teammates.' She paused and calmed herself. 'Dear God, what sort of life have you had to make you so horribly suspicious?'

The question rocked him. He was, he realised, as influenced by the inevitable secrecy and suspicion of his work for the Mystiko Kataskopos as he was by the stillness and silence of his meditation. He wasn't just a prayerful lover of God, he was also a man who killed in His name – a man trained and encouraged to do so by others who claimed they shared his devotion.

Raphael couldn't stop memories of his work from flashing through his mind. They were filled with blood and death and corruption. When he was not at home working with Gemma and the dogs, he was engaged in the darkest aspects of human behaviour. He was the most successful operative in the MK precisely because he was the most suspicious, the most manipulative, the most skilled at plotting and killing.

Dear God, who had he become?

Raphael stared straight ahead. His eyes pierced the darkness; a part of him wished they didn't.

25

'Why won't you answer me?' Cat's voice pulled him back to the present.

The obvious answer would have been, 'Because I don't trust you.' Only that didn't feel right now. Instead he said, 'I'm the best at what I do, and there's always a price to pay in becoming the best.'

'What price have you paid?'

'More than I knew.'

She was quiet for a moment then she said, 'Mack told me you killed Eddie. He said you executed him in cold blood.'

Raphael looked towards her. 'He had his own reasons for telling you that.'

'But why did you do it? You said Eddie had told you everything you wanted to know. So why did you feel the need to...?'

'I went back to confirm that Eddie was at least involved in your brother's death, and to do what was necessary to keep you safe.'

'And?'

'He was, and I couldn't.'

'Couldn't what?'

'Do what was necessary for your protection. Eddie was going to come after you and your family from the first minute he was free. I know how to disappear. I've got an organisation to protect me in ways the police can't protect you. You were the vulnerable one, not me.'

'But if you'd told me you were going to kill Eddie, I would have told you not to do it.'

'That's why I didn't tell you, that and the fact that I wanted to spare you the burden. Anyway it's irrelevant, because I didn't do it. Logistically, I should have, but I just couldn't make myself. So I prayed for Eddie and left him just as I'd found him.'

'Then why did Mack tell me you'd killed him?'

'Either to trick you into something. Or...'

'What is it?'

'Or because someone else paid Eddie a visit after me and did what I couldn't.'

'Is that possible?'

'He would have made plenty of enemies. Maybe one of them just got lucky. Unlike you and me.'

'What do you mean?'

'Although you had obviously been seen by the barman, I didn't realise that Eddie had cameras operating in his flat. I should have checked when we were first there. That was a schoolboy error.'

'For someone who says they're the best at what they do?'

'I haven't been operating at my best on this mission.'

'Why not?'

'Because of you! As I told you, I'm used to working alone.'

She considered for a moment. 'Right at the beginning, when you got me to follow you into the pub, what was your intention?'

'It wasn't for it to turn out like this.'

'That's you ducking a question again.'

'Yes.'

They lapsed into silence.

Eventually she asked, 'Were you planning to kill me?'

'I wasn't planning anything; I was exploring options.'

'Was killing me one of those options?'

'Options are just identified possibilities,' he said. 'Ultimately, actions are what matter most and given that I couldn't bring myself to kill Eddie, I'd say you were pretty safe from the very beginning.'

'Thank you,' she said after another pause.

'What for?'

'Wanting to protect my family and me.'

'I haven't done too good a job of it so far.'

'I still believe in you.' She looked at him through the darkness. 'Do you believe me now when I say that I'm not working for Swann?'

'Yes.' He saw her body relax. His didn't. If she hadn't betrayed him, there was only one option left. It was the worst one. He still didn't want to believe that.

'What is the organisation you work for?' She asked.

'I can't tell you,' he replied. 'Other than to say I believe it to be the most important organisation in the world, that its history and purpose are beyond reproach.'

'How come you're saying such an amazing thing, but you sound so unsure? There was a hesitancy in your voice I haven't heard before.'

'Maybe you're reading too much into it.' He forced a smile, hoping his voice would lighten.

'No. You can't put me off that easily. I might be a relatively inexperienced detective, but I know when a person is showing signs of uncertainty. What's caused yours?'

'I don't remember admitting to any.'

CHRIS PARKER

'The way you spoke about your organisation, it was distanced as if you've realised something has changed.'

Raphael said nothing.

'It's the people, isn't it?' Cat said suddenly. 'After all, an organisation is simply a collection of people working together. And people make mistakes or develop their own agenda. At their worst, they corrupt parts of the organisation they work for. It's happened at times in the police force, it happens everywhere. Your organisation can't be any different!'

'It ought to be,' he said. 'I need it to be.'

'How can a man with your training be so naive?'

'I don't see it as naivety.'

'What do you see it as?'

'Faith,' he said simply.

They both heard the sound of the lift at the same time.

It stopped them talking. The two men who had brought Raphael down entered the room. One stayed by the lift as the other approached him.

'The Boss wants to see you,' he said. 'You're being given an audience that few get.' He pulled him to his feet. 'Sooner you than me.'

Raphael let his body slump, feigning weakness as the man moved him. He ignored Cat completely. He sensed she was about to say something but stopped herself. He had no choice but to leave her alone in the darkness. As the lift door closed, he prepared himself for the imminent challenge of the light.

26

The two men didn't speak to him or each other. When they reached ground level they marched him, grim-faced, into the study he had observed through his scope. Sir Desmond Swann was sitting in a low-backed leather armchair. His legs were crossed. The sole of his upraised shoe was unmarked. Raphael remembered his handler.

Those shoes have never walked the streets.

Swann gestured to the empty chair opposite him. The men placed Raphael in it. Swann dismissed them with a wave of his right hand. He waited until they had closed the door behind them before speaking.

'Mr Ward,' he said. 'It is a pleasure to meet you. It is a pleasure because it means you are finally under my control. That, in case you haven't realised it, is the natural order of things. I either own or I control. I find both easy and enjoyable. You see, wielding power is similar to lifting weights. You adapt by becoming stronger, and the stronger you become the more weight you are capable of lifting and holding. Inevitably your grip becomes greater and you hold onto more and more with increasing ease. Of course, when you choose to let things go they fall with a crash that can affect others.' He smiled. 'Sometimes, though, when I let things go no one notices. Apart from those directly involved.' He smiled again. 'Do you think you will be noticed?'

'I don't think that matters one way or another.' Raphael looked over the billionaire's shoulders. He saw how the tweed two-piece suit he was wearing hung on his slim frame. He saw the heavy, gold cufflinks showing below the jacket sleeves, the streaks of grey in his thick black hair, and most of all, the quiet arrogance of a man who regarded the world as his plaything. 'And I don't think you've ever lifted a weight in your life.'

Swann chuckled. 'So you enjoy being the grey man? You enjoy being unnoticed, the man who doesn't even really exist?'

'If I don't exist who are you talking to?'

'I'm talking to a failure wrapped in human form. I'm talking to a man with no identity and no hope. I'm talking to an example of the limited, easily controlled, short-sighted mass who make up ninety-nine point nine per cent of the world's population. In short, I'm talking to no one special.'

'Then why are you giving me your time? Why don't you just hand me over to Mack so that he can avenge his brother?'

'Everything has its time and place, Mr Ward. I'm sure you believe that. And your time with Mack will come. Right now, I want to share some things with you – one in particular. I want to ensure that, before you die, you understand precisely just who and what I am.'

'Do you think I don't know that?'

'I think there are many things you don't know.'

'I'm sure you will enlighten me.'

'Men like you cannot be enlightened. It is not within your capability. If it was, you would have already realised the most obvious of all things.'

Swann spoke in a slow, carefully modulated tone. It was a

sign, Raphael decided, of the value the man placed on his own intellect and power.

He enjoys listening to himself talk.

'And what, pray, is the most obvious of all things?'

Swann sighed. 'It has nothing to do with prayer, Mr Ward. Rather it is reflection of a Psalm. It's Psalm eighty-nine verse eleven to be precise. You know it perhaps?'

'Why do you think that?'

'Please,' Swann wiped invisible bits of fluff from his trouser, 'let's not play games. I know who you are, where you are from and why you are here. It is inconceivable that a man with your background cannot recite that Psalm.'

'You're right.' Raphael ran his eyes over the bookshelf at the far end of the study. 'The Psalm reads, "The heavens are yours; the earth also is yours; the world and all that is in it, you have founded them."'

'Very good!' Swann beamed. 'I knew you wouldn't disappoint me.'

'So far you're disappointing me.'

'I very much doubt it.' Swann pushed his glasses further up his nose. 'Yet even if I am, that will change as we progress our conversation. However, for the moment let's return to the very obvious truth of the Psalm, which is simply this: man owns everything. Man has built this world in his own image. Men of power walk this earth as the ultimate creators. The writer of the Psalm knew this. It has been the most obvious truth throughout history.'

Raphael laughed. It was a brief, harsh sound. 'Men like you destroy this world; you are the creators of nothing but the world's pain.' He flexed his hands, feeling the metal of the handcuffs against his wrists. 'As you like to misinterpret Scripture, let me share a verse that even you cannot corrupt. It's from Paul's First Epistle to the Corinthians, chapter four verse two. It reads: "Moreover, it is required of stewards that they be found trustworthy." Men with your so-called power are the stewards of our planet, not the creators. Yet you betray the trust placed in you, in pursuit of your own greed.'

'And you wish to kill me in the name of a loving God.' Swann absent-mindedly turned the signet ring around his finger. 'But as there is no such thing as a loving God and, as you are my prisoner, I don't need to concern myself with either.' He looked at Raphael. 'Have you been so successful – until today – because of your skill or because you have just been lucky?'

'Successful at what?'

'And still you want to play,' Swann chuckled. 'Your body reflects your training; your words reveal both the indoctrination you have been subjected to and your child-like acceptance of its tenets. To me, Mr Ward, you are not the grey man. I see you clearly. I know you completely. The fact that I captured you so easily is proof of that.'

'You didn't capture me. Others did.'

'Men I own, men who do my bidding willingly and without question. There are so many of them, Mr Ward. I feed their pockets, I buy them trinkets, I give them a pin-head of power, and as one, they work to my design.'

'Which one of them told you about me?'

'Ah!' Swann inclined his head briefly. 'Ultimately those insights came from a friend, not an employee. You see the greatest secret of them all is that, for those of us who possess real power, there are no secrets. We know everything.

'Secrets exist within the mass. We plant them there. They are part of the glue that holds the ninety-nine point nine per cent together. Secrets are the basis for your stories, your fears, your beliefs and your hopes. Secrets drain away the energy of the mass and consume their time. 'For people like me, however, everything is accessible; everything is shared. My friend exercises a power similar to mine. We view things from the same perspective. That is all you need to know.'

'A shared perspective doesn't ensure clarity.'

'From where I stand no organisation can remain secret, not even the Mystiko Kataskopos.' Swann clapped his hands together. 'Do you understand now?'

Raphael blinked. Cat's words came back to him.

'People make mistakes or develop their own agenda. At their worst, they corrupt parts of the organisation they work for.'

Option three – the one he had dreaded – was indeed true. Someone inside the MK was helping Swann. Now, more than ever before Raphael felt truly alone.

'No one has ever betrayed the MK,' he said.

'No one has ever been caught betraying the MK,' Swann corrected. 'And I am sure that no one ever will be.'

'I don't know what to say,' Raphael shook his head. 'That is the most appropriate response,' Swann said. 'When one finally realises that their worldview is flawed and their belief system false, the only honest reaction is to submit to the reality around them.'

Raphael flexed his hands again against the handcuffs. 'Now that you have finally come to appreciate the hopelessness of your situation, it is time for us to move on to the one special thing I want to share with you. After all, it would be unfair in the extreme to deny you the honour of experiencing my ultimate possession before you die.' Swann stood up. 'But first the story that goes with it, a story devoid of secrets, the true story of what you call the *SS*.'

Despite his sense of despair, Raphael could not stop his heartbeat from quickening. He straightened in his seat. He knew that excitement and curiosity were showing on his face and he didn't care.

Swann saw the effect of his words and nodded

encouragingly. 'I know how much this means to you,' he said. 'I know that early in its history the Roman Catholic Church established a secret sect of elite spies and killers tasked with protecting the Church, its secrets and its treasures. Over the centuries this sect also worked to recover religious artefacts and artwork stolen by others. In more recent times there has been a specific focus on retrieving those objects taken by the Nazis between 1940 and 1945.

'Peter, the first Leader of the Church, had to name this group. His first decision was to choose the language. Members of the early Church used both Greek and Aramaic, so he had to determine which would be the most appropriate going forwards. Peter decided it was Greek. He called your forebears the Mystiko Kataskopos. Mystiko, meaning 'secret' and Kataskopos literally meaning 'a looking down', with its more common interpretation being 'spy' or 'scout'. As I have already intimated Mr Ward, or whoever you really are, I do know all about the Mystiko Kataskopos.

'Over the centuries the name has been shortened, apart from in the most formal of circumstances, so you now refer to yourselves as the MK. Personally I find it a tragedy that your organisation has acquiesced to the trend of reducing everything down to its most simplistic. It's a form of laziness that underpins much of what is wrong in our world. And it is particularly strange and sad that such an active body as the Mystiko Kataskopos should fall into that trap. After all, Mr Ward, you and your fellows are incredibly disciplined and rigorous in your training. You are the Church's own select army of contemplative monks, adept in both mystical practices and the dark arts of spying and assassination.'

Swann leant forwards. 'I can't help but think it's fitting that, as a monk, you spend so much of your time in a cell, and if your crimes were discovered by the so-called Authorities, they would send you immediately to their own version!'

'I'm not a criminal.'

'Sadly, we don't have time to debate that. Suffice to say, that if you were ever arrested the Church would look the other way and you, out of a misguided sense of loyalty, would not reveal your true identity or your motives. However, it is a moot point. You are never going to be arrested, I guarantee you of that.'

Raphael shrugged. 'You were going to tell me about your relationship with the *SS*,' he said.

'Yes,' Swann smiled. 'Your urgency and desire are palpable. Your need to know is greater, it seems, than any fear of your impending death. So, let me share with you the full and accurate history of La Santa Sindone, the object you refer to as *SS*, the object I possess, the object known to most as the Shroud of Turin.

27

———

Swann rose to his feet, as if beginning a lecture.

'The Shroud is a rectangular length of linen cloth, over fourteen feet long and three feet wide. It is believed by millions to be the cloth in which the body of Jesus of Nazareth was wrapped after his crucifixion. What is most startling about the Shroud is that it actually bears the negative image of the front and back of a naked man with his hands folded across his groin.

'His height cannot be determined accurately, but many experts believe it to be five feet seven inches or perhaps a little more. He has a beard, moustache and shoulder-length hair. There are also reddish-brown stains on the cloth, showing a number of wounds he appears to have received. These wounds, believers argue, correlate with the injuries Jesus suffered.

'If the Shroud of Turin is the genuine sindone, or burial cloth of Jesus, it is quite simply the most important and valuable object on the planet. It is as close as we could ever come to proving that the death and resurrection of Jesus are historical facts; the image having been somehow imprinted on the material at the instance of his miraculous victory over death. It follows then, that the question of its authenticity is the single most important question of all time. To answer it fully we need to know something about the history of the Shroud.

'Unfortunately, there are few reliable historical records concerning the Shroud prior to the fourteenth century. It does not mean, though, that what there is should be ignored.

'For example, as early as the second century, there is a reference in what remains of The Gospel of the Hebrews that reads, "and after He had given the linen cloth to the servant of the priest he appeared to James". This, of course, proves nothing other than the fact that some form of linen cloth relating to Jesus was in public discourse.

'In the early fourth century, it is recorded that King Abgar of Edessa had written to Jesus asking him to visit and cure him of an illness. Jesus refused the request, but one of his disciples, Thaddeus, eventually visited in his place and the King was miraculously cured. A portrait showing the face of Jesus on a rectangular cloth was also brought to Edessa and stored in the royal palace. In 593AD Evagrius Scholasticus wrote about this, saying the picture was of divine origin.

'For centuries the Image of Edessa has been regarded as a most important holy relic and the first icon. Some have even suggested there is a connection between the Image and the Shroud, and a few have gone so far as to argue that they are one and the same. They base their belief on the apocryphal Acts of Thaddeus, written around the same time, that claims the cloth was folded into four pieces so that only the face was visible. According to this tradition the cloth was moved to Constantinople in the tenth century.

'And, in 1204, a knight named Robert de Clari who fought in the Fourth Crusade and spent time in the captured city of Constantinople, claimed that the cloth was among the countless relics found there. Writings attributed to de Clari included the following reference: "There was the Shroud in which our Lord had been wrapped, which every Friday raised itself upright so one could see the figure of our Lord on it. And none knows – neither Greek nor Frank – what became of that shroud when the city was taken."'

Swann sniffed and adjusted his glasses. 'Personally I subscribe to the view that the suggested miracle of the cloth raising itself can be disregarded in favour of a simple mistranslation of the text. Anyone with an appropriate level of education would know that the French impersonal passive takes the form of a reflexive verb. Therefore, de Clari's original French could be translated equally well to read the cloth "was raised upright". I would suggest this is almost certainly the case, as there is nothing in his writing that implies he experienced anything miraculous. Regardless of that, the Shroud apparently disappeared soon afterwards.

'We are obliged, therefore, to move forwards one hundred and fifty years for our next insight, when historical records indicate that a shroud bearing an image of a crucified man was in the possession of a knight called Geoffroy de Charny. He lived in the small town of Lirey in France. According to the records, after he died his widow displayed the Shroud in the local church. At the time, this caused a mixed and significant response from the Church. Since then, many researchers have argued that the Lirey cloth was the work of a forger.'

Swann looked quizzically at Raphael. 'What is your opinion?'

Raphael feigned disinterest. 'You told me you were going to share a story devoid of secrets and that you knew the truth of La Santa Sindone,' he said. 'Yet so far you all you have done is report a mix of well-known facts, questionable hypotheses and popular myths. There is nothing you have said that makes me think you have an exceptional level of knowledge, let alone that you have insights only a person of power could possess.'

'You are trying to bait me,' Swann patted Raphael's shoulder. 'It is a futile exercise. And I am, indeed, going to demonstrate a level of knowledge not even you will expect. Let's move our story on a bit, shall we?' Swann moved away and began to pace the room.

'In 1532, the Shroud suffered damage from a fire in the chapel where it was stored. Nuns dealt with this as best they could, putting patches onto the damaged material. In 1578 the House of Savoy took the Shroud to Turin. It was not shown to the public for nearly a hundred years.

'In 1694 it was placed in the specially constructed Guarini Chapel, known in Italian as Cappella della Sacra Sindone, the Chapel of the Holy Shroud. As centuries passed the validity of the Shroud was questioned continually, but nothing dampened its impact on believers.

'In 1918, towards the end of the First World War, a special underground chamber was built to house the Shroud and protect it during air raids. The casket in which the Shroud lay was wrapped in asbestos and put in a chest made of tin plate. This is significant because in 1972 someone tried to destroy the Shroud by setting fire to it. They failed due to the asbestos protection.

'Five years later, in 1977, scientists at Rochester University in New York State began experimenting with the accelerator mass spectrometry method of radiocarbon dating. It is a method that allowed much smaller samples of material to be tested than had previously been possible. This too is significant because this would be the method used in 1988 to carbon date the Shroud.

'Gaining permission to carry out these tests was a lengthy and troublesome affair. In 1986 scientists named seven laboratories they wished to take part in the testing. They forwarded this list and their proposed protocol to the Pope and the Cardinal of Turin. Their proposal was rejected. Instead the

Church offered them the opportunity to carry out a scaled-down experiment involving only three laboratories. The lead scientists made clear their concerns about the validity of such limited tests, but the Church stood firm. It was going to be, as some would say, their way or the highway.' Swann chuckled. 'Which takes us back to the natural order of things. Those who have power determine the behaviour of those who don't.

'Anyway, the scientists decided to go ahead and laboratories in Arizona, Zurich and Oxford went to work. By August 1988 all testing was done. On October 13th of the same year, Cardinal Ballestrero, the Archbishop of Turin, announced to the press that the scientists had dated the Shroud between 1260 and 1390AD. Simply put, it was a fake. What we might now regard as the first and, arguably, the biggest example of fake news the world has ever known. In fact, in 1990 the British Museum held an exhibition titled "Fake. The Art of Deception" which included a full-size transparency of the Shroud.

'Incredibly, though, as the years have passed the facts haven't swayed the beliefs of the faithful. How do you feel about that, Mr Ward?'

'I also have my own beliefs,' Raphael said. 'And you know as well as I do that there are scientists who argue the methods used in 1988 lacked rigour, that the samples tested came from a rewoven area of the Shroud that was not part of the original cloth.'

'Claim and counter-claim,' Swann said. 'But the truth is, we both know that it all counts for nothing. Don't we?' He winked. 'You really were hoping that I was full of bluster and bluff, weren't you? I'm afraid I possess neither. I know as much about the Shroud of Turin as any man alive. And I know, as you do, that in 1988 the Church chose to provide the scientists with a sindone they knew to be a fourteenth century forgery.'

28

Raphael closed his eyes and sank back in the chair. Swann clearly hadn't been lying when he had boasted about his level of knowledge. Someone had shared with him one of the Church's greatest secrets. The many disruptions and delays in agreeing to the carbon dating had been created for one, simple reason: the Church knew what the result would be. The Shroud they had been putting on public display since October 1946, when it had been exhibited to the monks of Montevergine, was a fake.

'The Church had no choice,' Raphael said quietly. 'The Shroud of Turin is real. It is the very shroud Jesus' uncle, Joseph of Arimathea, bought and wrapped his holy body in. It does bear the genuine imprint of the resurrected Christ. It is the most holy object on Earth.'

'And the Church had it and lost it,' Swann said. 'I know the true story behind the fake news.' He sat down, facing Raphael. 'I know that on the first of July 1935 Heinrich Himmler who was, in a most gloriously ironic twist, the head of the Nazi SS, created the Ahnenerbe, more commonly known as the Ancestral Heritage Research and Teaching Organisation.

'Whilst that title makes the group sound relatively harmless, nothing could be further from the truth. The word Ahnenerbe literally means "Inheritance of the Forefathers". It was an extremely well-funded paranormal research group supported fully by the Führer. The Ahnenerbe logo itself featured rune-style lettering, in the belief that this would invoke the power of the magical shapes.

'Hitler, Himmler and many other leading Nazi figures were interested in the occult, arguably to the point of obsession. The Nazi Party had actually begun as an occult fraternity. It was only later that it transformed into a political entity. Given that, it's not surprising that Himmler's SS was heavily influenced by occult beliefs. Their headquarters, the castle of Wewelsburg, was even modelled on Arthurian legend.

'The Nazis also used psychics and astrologers to attack enemy forces in ways that the military could not. Strategies were developed based on the alignment of the planets. The Ahnenerbe sent expeditions all over the world in search of objects with magical and mystical powers. Everyone knows that during the Second World War the Nazis stole many great artworks. Few know that they were even more committed to their search for occult power.

'They sent teams to Tibet, looking for traces of the original, uncorrupted Aryan race; to Ethiopia in search of the Ark of the Covenant; to France for the Holy Grail; to Iceland to find the secret gateway into a magical land populated by telepathic giants which, Hitler believed, was the original home of Aryans. The hope was, that by gaining entrance to this place, the Nazis could speed up their Aryan breeding programme and produce superhumans.

'If the Nazis were prepared to invest so heavily in searching for mystical objects and places that were lost, it is no surprise that Nazi Propaganda Minister Joseph Goebbels, along with Himmler, decided to steal the original, genuine Shroud of Turin. After all, they knew precisely where it was. The only challenge was getting it.

'They put their idea to Hitler. He saw it as a stroke of genius and ordered that it be prioritized, second only to the Icelandic search. Given the nature of the Führer, however, such enthusiastic support brought with it a very grave risk. The mission had to be successful or heads would roll. Hitler, like all great men, was not famous for his tolerance of failure.'

Swann sat down. He crossed his legs and entwined his fingers on his lap. 'It pains me to confess – and in the ongoing spirit of revelation, I am going to confess – that I do not know what the actual plan was, or who carried it out. My source has never been keen to share with me quite how the Church managed to lose its most prized possession to the Nazis. I suspect it is too great a source of embarrassment. Those details are, though, secondary to the fact that Goebbels and Himmler were successful. The Shroud was stolen. Hitler rejoiced. The Church could not, and has never since been able to, acknowledge the theft.

'There are only five things we subsequently know to be true. Firstly, that possession of the Shroud failed to help the Nazis win the war. Secondly, that somehow the Nazis, in turn, also lost the Shroud. Thirdly, that the MK has been searching for it without success since its original disappearance. Fourthly, that the Church was eventually forced into providing one of the several fakes it owns to be carbon tested.'

Swann fell silent.

Raphael took the bait. 'And fifthly?'

Swann beamed. 'That I own the genuine Shroud. That is why you are here. Your mission, as a good member of the MK, like any well-trained dog, is to retrieve it and take it home to your master. Unfortunately for you, my source doesn't want that to happen.'

Raphael said, 'I don't understand why someone in the MK, someone who is a part of the Church, would not want the Shroud to come home.'

'Of course you don't. Why should you? The dog doesn't understand why it's been given the command; it just does as it's told. If it finds itself in a trap en route, sooner or later it will bite its own leg off in a desperate attempt to escape.' Swann pretended to peer over Raphael's shoulders. 'Have you been doing any tugging and pulling against the handcuffs yet?'

'I know better than to waste my energy.'

'Good boy.'

'I'm not yours to command.'

'That's irrelevant now, wouldn't you say? Your timespan is increasingly limited. I will auction the Shroud tomorrow to twelve of the most powerful individuals on the planet. I invited twelve because it seemed the most appropriate number.'

Raphael ignored the other's smile. 'How did you come to acquire the Shroud? Even for a man with your connections and authority, it can't have been easy.'

'Ha-Ha!' Swann laughed. 'You can't really believe that I'm going to tell you more than I already have? Suffice it to say that at this moment in time, I own the Shroud and I own you. And in a little over twenty-four hours from now, I'm going to have profited enormously from the most discreet and significant auction of all time. Before then, although I won't answer your question, I am going to provide you with the most amazing experience of your solitary life.'

'You have no idea what experiences I might have had.'

'Alone in the darkness of your cell?' Swann smirked. 'I assure you it will be nothing like this.' He rose to his feet.

'Stand up.' Raphael did.

Swann led them to his bookshelf. He gestured towards it with his right hand. 'Now,' he said, 'before you die I am going to show you the real Shroud of Turin.'

29

S wann removed the same book Raphael had seen him go to before. The monk could see a button on the wall. Swann pressed it. The bookshelf opened, the two halves moving apart to reveal a security door with an electronic locking mechanism. Swann keyed in the code and the heavy door eased opened. They stepped into a steel lined secure room that Raphael estimated to be at least twenty feet long, twelve feet wide and eighteen feet to the ceiling. A heavy, dark green, velvet drape covered the far wall.

Swann closed the door behind them. It locked automatically. Raphael felt as if he was inside a very large safe.

'Stay where you are,' Swann said. 'And prepare to come face-to-face with the man you call the Christ.' He pointed a remote control at the drape. The material began to slide apart along the gold motorised rails from which it hung. Swann stepped to one side, watching Raphael's face rather than the theatrical reveal.

The monk was transfixed. His heart was pounding. La Santa Sindone, the genuine burial shroud of Jesus, the physical manifestation of the resurrection, was here!

It seemed to Raphael that the heavy velvet material was

moving in slow motion. He was only vaguely aware of Swann saying, 'Like the parting of the seas for Moses and the Israelites.' He was only vaguely aware that he was still a prisoner. His sense of mission was forgotten completely.

Then, suddenly, there it was! Everything he had spent his life searching for.

The image hung on the wall. Raphael felt as if it was staring down at him.

The almost hollow face with the beard, moustache and long hair.

Hands folded over the groin.

The reddish-brown stains showing wounds that were unique to the crucifixion of Jesus.

Raphael couldn't help but think of the suffering they represented.

The crown of thorns, pressed down into the scalp, drawing blood, in a mocking response to claims of Kingship.

The spear thrust driven up into the torso, delivered to speed up his death; to ensure the body was removed before the Passover began. It had pierced the pericardial sac causing the release of a transparent fluid much like water, before the inevitable flow of blood.

The heavy iron nails, probably eight inches long, hammered through both wrists to ensure the body could not fall from the cross. Hammered, too, through the feet, breaking bones, causing further extreme distress.

Raphael could not help but step back a pace. An unwanted, uncomfortable feeling was stirring inside him. He tried to dismiss it but failed. Swann spoke again. Raphael tried to use the sound of his words to shake the growing sense that something was terribly wrong.

'It's magnificent, isn't it?' Swann glanced at the Shroud. 'What is so fascinating is the historical accuracy of the wounds.

I'm sure you appreciate that. Most people think, for example, that Jesus was nailed through the hands – presumably because so many great artists have painted it that way. That simply wouldn't have worked, of course. As the body weakened and slumped, the iron nails would have simply ripped through the skin and bones and the body would have tumbled. No self-respecting Roman soldier would have allowed that to happen. It would have shown incompetency, and it would have meant they had to spend time fastening the victim back up. No, if you were going to use nails they had to go in through the wrists because the bones there would hold steady against the increasing pull of the body.

'The spear thrust is also interesting. Crucifixion was designed to be a slow death and a deterrent to others. A reasonably healthy individual would last anything up to thirty-six hours before they finally gave out. And it wasn't the pain that killed them. Asphyxiation was the most common cause of death, but dehydration and exposure could do it too.

'The thing is, Jesus lasted only about six hours. Now, admittedly, they were in a rush because of the impending festival and the need to get all the bodies down and out of the way before that started, but the Romans usually broke their victims' legs if they wanted to speed up crucifixion. They were, after all, masters of punishment. Breaking someone legs ensured another huge dose of pain whilst taking away their support structure.

'That was the fun of crucifixion, the person tired, the body slumped, they'd struggle to breath and, until the very end, they'd keep finding the strength in their legs to push themselves back up. Once they were straight, or at least close to it, they'd get a few in-breaths of good old oxygen before they'd weaken again. Up and down, in and out, time after time until they just couldn't do it anymore. Once you broke their legs, however, they were going to asphyxiate very quickly.

'Only Jesus didn't get the old hammer across the knees. He got the practically unheard-of spear in the side, thanks to a centurion who, for some reason, wanted to do him a favour. He was a lucky chap, wouldn't you say?'

Raphael couldn't take his eyes away from the linen. 'It's the image,' he said slowly. 'It's the image.'

'Of course it's the image,' Swann frowned. 'It's only ever been about the image.'

'It's so feint,' Raphael murmured. 'It's barely visible.'

'That's because it's the genuine object and not some forger's artwork,' Swann snapped. 'Don't tell me you're disappointed?'

Raphael shook his head. The feeling inside him was almost unbearable; the questions in his mind were so loud he could barely hear Swann speak.

Why am I not on my knees? Why am I not weeping?

'You look like you're in shock,' Swann said.

Raphael bit his lip and tasted blood. He forced himself to ask, 'How do you know this is the real Shroud? Have you had it carbon tested?'

'I didn't need to. I know everything there is to know about the genuine sindone, remember? I'm the expert here. I know the complete history of this particular object. And that is what matters most. Regardless of what you or anyone else might think, the Shroud is essentially nothing more than a work of art, and in the art world provenance is everything. I can prove the provenance of this beyond doubt. The would-be buyers attending my auction are all assured of this, and none of them want to damage even the tiniest part of the cloth to let science verify what I already know.'

Raphael heard the words as if from a distance. He felt a

vacuum in his chest, emptiness in his soul. He felt as if he was falling through space, but his eyes told him that was not so.

'You're mistaken in so many ways,' he said, unsure just whom he was talking to.

'You're wrong!' Swann replied angrily. 'I have ownership and that is all that matters.'

'We own nothing,' Raphael said, as tears filled his eyes for all the wrong reasons.

30

Mack was waiting for them in the study. As the bookshelf closed, hiding its secret, he handed Swann a sheet of A5 paper. The billionaire read it swiftly. He nodded curtly.

'That's good. Everything is in place and going as planned.' He screwed the paper up, dropped it into a large ashtray and set fire to it using a golden cigarette lighter.

'In some ways paper is a far more useful commodity than technology,' he said to Raphael as the message blackened and charred in the flames. 'The encouragement to avoid paper in favour of phones, tablets, computers and the like is a ploy. It is designed and employed by those of us who seek to gain insights into the behaviours and emotional preferences of the powerless majority.

'Paper disintegrates and its information goes with it. A person's technological footprint is almost impossible to erase, and most people leave a trail that is all-too easy to follow. There is, I find, a wonderful and endearing irony in the way that companies persuade people who can't afford it, to spend increasing amounts on the latest technology, so that people like me can influence them more easily.'

'Perhaps if you turned your attention inwards instead of on everyone else you might...' Raphael's voice trailed off as the desire to speak disappeared into the emptiness that had overtaken him.

He had expected the real Shroud to fill his heart, to be the most powerful of all religious experiences, a mystical encounter that destroyed and freed in equal measure. He had imagined it would somehow draw together past and present, collapse all boundaries and bring forth a consciousness of connectivity and unity greater than any form of man-made division. Instead it had seemed distant, remote and lifeless; an object from another time that had lost any meaning it might once have had.

Was this the price he had paid for killing so many? Did the Shroud not touch him because he was no longer worthy? Did it not reveal itself because spiritually he was too blind to see?

Swann looked at his Head of Security. 'I fear our guest was somewhat underwhelmed by our auction item. I can't help but wonder if he has lost his faith.'

'It hardly makes a difference, does it?' Mack's voice was cold.

'In terms of his immediate future it makes no difference at all, but it does surprise me. For a man like him to lose his conviction, to seem so hollowed out, is as unexpected and, frankly, as unlikely as you suddenly choosing to forgive him for your brother's death.'

'That won't happen in this lifetime or the next.' Mack's eyes glittered.

'I recognise that look,' Swann acknowledged. He faced Raphael. 'It's the look that says he really doesn't want to wait any longer and, I'm sorry to inform you, he doesn't need to. Our time together is over. If it is any consolation, this was a mission you could never hope to accomplish. There were just too many people working against you, too many unknowns. Talking of which, that is where you will be heading shortly – into the great unknown.' He turned back to his employee. 'He's all yours. Please do make sure you stick to the time limit. In the grand scheme of things he still isn't as important as tomorrow's business.'

'I understand.' Mack took hold of Raphael's upper right arm. His grip was vice-like. 'Let's go.'

Raphael offered no resistance. He paid no heed to the route they took through the mansion. The Mystiko Kataskopos had been corrupted. He had lost his soul. Only his body remained and he had no desire to save it.

Mack opened a solid wooden door and pushed him inside. The walls were bare. The floor was covered in a thick plastic tarpaulin. There was a single chair placed in the centre of the room. Mack pushed him into it.

'If you ever wondered where you would die,' Mack said, 'this is the place. It's been here waiting for you for all these years. Strange isn't it, all those countries you've visited doing your work, all the different places you've met people, all the shadows and the dark streets, all the locked doors and secret meetings, and it all comes down to this.' He gestured deliberately. 'A bare room in a building filled with treasures. Just you, me and a carpet for your blood.'

Mack drove the first two knuckles of his right fist hard into Raphael's left ear. The blow knocked both the man and the chair sideways. Raphael grunted involuntarily as his head rocked violently.

Mack waited for the effects of the blow to subside before speaking again. 'I rarely punch people,' he said, 'and I never do if they're a moving target. It's too easy to damage your own hand. Don't you agree?'

Raphael said nothing. The ringing in his ear was loud, the pain still significant. He knew that Mack had measured the force of the strike deliberately. If it had been much harder it would have damaged the eardrum and almost certainly knocked him out. That was the last thing his captor wanted.

'I prefer to slap someone if I have to hit to the head with my hands,' Mack went on. 'This usually works.' He jabbed the heel of his palm into the centre of Raphael's forehead, jolting the head backwards. The monk felt the inevitable shock as his brain bounced inside his skull, hitting the bone.

'Like a large, bouncy ball in a small space, eh?' Mack grinned. 'Jelly on a plate, my old instructor used to call it.' He showed his open right palm and tapped the lower part with the fingertips of his left hand. 'It's not really the hand that does the damage; it's the end of the forearm bone that connects if you do it properly. You only need a half-decent strike to cause loss of consciousness. Actually, it takes more skill to just shake someone around a bit, than it does to knock them out.'

Mack moved to Raphael's left shoulder. 'You don't always need to use the bone,' he said. 'If you choose your target correctly, you only need to cup your palm. Like this!'

He snapped his hand against the base of Raphael's skull, causing him to blink and gasp. The monk felt as if he was teetering on the edge of a dark abyss. Then Mack's voice drew him back.

'It's a version of the good, old-fashioned rabbit punch,' he said, 'so-called because poachers and hunters kill rabbits by using a swift blow to the back of the neck. If you haven't worked it out, you're the rabbit in my headlights. I just don't want to kill you yet.' He stepped back in front of Raphael. He was holding the monk's knife in his hand. 'My boys took this off you. They knew I'd be interested in it.'

Mack raised the curved blade and made a few, slow passes with it in front of Raphael's face. 'Whilst I know how to disable or kill using only my bare hands,' he said, 'my real passion is for the blade. I've been attracted to them ever since I was a boy. I have quite a collection. I don't have one of these, though.' Mack studied the weapon. 'It's a modern version of a Sica, isn't it? When I was in Bosnia I heard that ancient Sica were found there occasionally, but I couldn't get my hands on one. It was a real shame.'

Raphael felt the first stirrings of emotion in his lower stomach as he watched Mack testing the balance of the knife. Pietro had given the Sica to him when he had completed his training. No one else had ever handled it.

'Imagine owning an original, a dagger that had been made at the time of the ancient Thracians,' Mack went on. 'Imagine how many lives it would have taken, how much blood it must have washed in. Don't get me wrong, this is good, it's clearly made by a craftsman,' he made several slashing movements in front of his chest, 'but the originals must be something else. Let's face it, they've even played their part in shaping history and language!'

Raphael glared at him. Mack appeared not to notice. 'The Sicarii, a Jewish faction violently opposed to the Roman occupation of Judaea, carried these daggers hidden in their cloaks,' he said. 'They were one of the first organised assassination units in history, operating well before the Islamic Hashishin and the Japanese ninja. Their very name came from the term Sicarius, or "dagger-man". Even today a Sicario in Spanish is a professional assassin.' Mack lowered the knife. 'Overall, then, it's the perfect weapon for you. Which makes it the perfect weapon for me to kill you with. But the final thrust is going to feel like it's a long time coming, I promise you that.'

Raphael inhaled deeply. He recognized the emotion now. It was anger. It was bringing life back with it. He spoke instinctively. 'What's going to happen to Cat?'

'Oh, so you do have some words left inside you.' Mack considered briefly. 'She is going to stay out of harm's way until our guests have been and gone. Then I'm going to hold an auction of my own, I'm going to auction her to my team. I won't mind if they bid singularly or in groups. The rules won't be as rigid as at Sir Desmond's auction. Anyway, the winning bid will get three hours of her time –it will be her last full three hours – after which I will use this,' he pointed with the Sica, 'to re-introduce her to her dead brother.'

The anger rushed through Raphael's body. He hoped it didn't show on his face.

'You need to make sure my knife doesn't kill you whilst you sleep,' he said.

'It's my hand holding it now!' Mack laughed, stepping forwards and lowering his face close to Raphael's. 'And it's you who's going to feel the blade.' He placed the knife's concave, cutting edge on the top of Raphael's left ear. 'I'm sure it's still throbbing with pain, so I'll cut it off for you. As long as you've got one good ear, you'll be able to hear yourself begging for me to end it.'

Raphael lowered his head, as if in defeat. In truth, the feel of the blade against his skin was energising him further. In his mind he heard Pietro's voice telling him to save Cat and complete the mission.

'I'm going to cut you apart, bit by bit,' Mack said, keeping his face low. 'Musashi wrote, "If the corners are overthrown, the spirit of the whole body will be overthrown". I'm going to overthrow your spirit before I kill your body.'

Raphael drove upwards from the chair without warning. He stamped his left foot onto Mack's right, pinning it in place. At the same time he slammed the top of his head into Mack's nose. He felt the bones shatter. Mack twisted and fell awkwardly. He was unconscious before he hit the floor. The Sica fell from his hand.

Raphael took a moment to regain his composure. Then he dropped to one knee and turned, sitting with his back to the other man's body. Just as he had hoped, the keys to the handcuffs were in Mack's pocket, along with his burner phone. It took only a few seconds to free himself.

Raphael picked up his knife and returned it to the sheath. He took Mack's phone and smashed it. Then he left the room, locking the door behind him.

31

Raphael moved swiftly along the corridor, searching for something that would help him get his bearings in the large home. He passed a closed door on his right and an instinct made him stop. A smile crossed his face as he studied the door. It was as solid and secure as the one he had just locked. It was there to keep someone in or to keep others out. It was either a prison or protection. Raphael was sure he knew which.

He knocked on the door; two confident blows in quick succession. The electronic lock buzzed quietly as the person inside gave him entry without question. Raphael's smile widened.

When moving through unknown perimeters, act as if you have been there a hundred times.

It was a lesson from many years ago. Over time, Raphael had added on to it,

And trust your instinct!

He opened the door and stepped inside as if he owned the room. It was, as he suspected, where the high-tech monitoring system was being operated. One man was sitting at the centre of a suite of desks. He was so engrossed in the numerous screens he was watching, he didn't turn round until it was too late.

Raphael jammed his inner left forearm across the man's lower face, forcing the bone into the base of his nose. The man jerked his head back, trying to get away from the pain. The move exposed his throat. Raphael's right arm snaked around the man's neck. He applied pressure to both carotid arteries, using his bodyweight to keep his victim seated. The man lost consciousness within seconds. Raphael released his grip and pushed the body onto the floor. He used the man's own belt to tie him. Then he gagged him using a pair of socks that were in a training bag underneath the desks.

Raphael spent the next five minutes studying all the images of the buildings and grounds that were showing on the screens. He compared these to the mental map he had memorised earlier. They matched perfectly. He took that to mean he was not suffering from concussion. He found where the lift was situated that went down to Cat's prison and then the stairs that went to the same place.

He set off for the stairs.

He was halfway down them before he heard the voices at the bottom. He guessed they were the two men who had taken him to meet Swann. He guessed they were intending to spend some time abusing Cat now, in case they lost the inevitable bidding war when the time came to auction her. He was sure they weren't expecting to see him again.

Raphael froze in place, waiting until the door to Cat's cell opened and the two men stepped inside. He heard one of them laugh. He forced himself to wait a few more seconds. He needed them to be completely absorbed with Cat. He had to trade her fear now, for her safety afterwards. Her voice raised suddenly. This time both men laughed.

Raphael made his move.

The men had switched the light on in the room. They were standing close to Cat, one on either side. They were staring at her. He might have reached them without being noticed, but his sudden appearance made Cat's eyes widen. The two men spun round. The one nearest to Raphael immediately launched an attack, moving forward, punching with his left hand.

Raphael raised his right elbow, deflecting the incoming blow and driving his elbow tip into the side of the man's jaw as the distance between them closed. He collapsed instantly.

Raphael continued the movement, spinning to his right, using the speed of his turn to throw a right backfist into the face of the second attacker. He caught him on the temple and raked the blow diagonally down, hitting both eye socket and nose. The man's forward momentum stopped dead.

Raphael lowered his stance, bringing his right palm back against the side of his own head, creating a natural battering ram with the point of his right elbow. He slammed it, without pausing, into the man's sternum. He felt the chest cave inwards as the fragile bone gave way. The man fell forwards, unconscious, gasping for air.

Raphael ignored him and freed Cat. He helped her to her feet. She was sobbing.

'We don't have time' he said, quietly and authoritatively. 'Your only hope is to get out of here quickly.'

Cat glanced down at the men. 'Are they...?'

He shook his head. 'No. I didn't kill them.'

'But...?'

He saw the confusion on her face. 'I seem to have lost the capacity for it,' he said. 'Even though I'm sure it's going to backfire at some point.'

She squeezed his arm. 'How do we get out?' She asked.

'You follow me,' he said. 'And once you're away from here,

keep going. This time, you really do have to follow my advice and find somewhere to hide for a while.'

She nodded. 'I understand.'

'But will you do it?'

'I promise.' She managed a smile. 'What are you going to do, once we're out?'

'I'm not leaving with you. I have to honour my commitment to my mission. Even though...'

'Even though, what?'

'Nothing.' He grabbed her hand. 'Whatever happens from now on, you have to keep going. Even if something happens to me, you have to get yourself safe. I need to know you'll do that. I can't do my job if a part of me is worrying about you.'

'I won't get in your way.'

'Then let's hope that I don't get in my way.'

'You won't,' she said, squeezing his hand reassuringly. 'How can you be so sure?' He asked.

'You're not the only one with faith,' she said.

They both raced upstairs.

32

He led her back to where the monitoring system was situated. The man he'd bound had regained consciousness and had tried unsuccessfully to use one of the phones on the desk. He backed away when he saw Raphael. The monk pointed to the corner of the room.

'Sit,' he ordered.

The man did as he was told.

Raphael promptly ignored him and scanned the monitors. Swann was still in his study. He could now see only three men in the grounds at the front of the mansion. There was one sitting in an armchair in the entrance hall. He was flicking through a magazine. There was no sign of Mack.

'Is that all of them?' Cat asked.

'It might be, but the thing is, we don't have to deal with all of them to get you out of here. In fact, we want to deal with as few as possible.'

'That would be good.'

'It certainly would.' Raphael cast his eyes over the technology for a final time. 'I've seen everything I need to, so we don't need this anymore.' He slid the Sica out of its sheath and cut every wire and cable. He used the butt of the handle to smash every screen. With that done, he took a step towards the corner and showed the razor-sharp blade to the man cowering there.

'I'm going to leave you. My friend will be here for a while longer. If she tells me that you've tried either to escape or contact someone, I will cut your throat wide open. Is that clear?' He leant forwards. The man nodded rapidly.

Raphael returned the knife to the sheath. He led Cat out into the corridor. 'You have to wait in that room for precisely three minutes after I leave,' he said. 'During that time you might hear some noise. There might even be gunfire. Even so, keep the door locked. Don't open it, even if someone comes knocking.'

'What about the guy inside?' Cat asked.

'Ignore him completely. I promise you, he will ignore you.'

'What do I do when the three minutes are up?'

'Leave, locking him in behind you. Then take the shortest, straightest route out: go through the main entrance and out to the drive. One of the vehicles there will be ready for you – it will be obvious which – jump in and drive away. Go to Maidenhead, ditch the car, and catch the first train back to London. From there, you're on your own. Pick a destination and tell no one. Just don't delay.'

'Ok.' Cat hesitated. 'How do you know I'll be able to leave like that?'

'I'm going to get the men who are there to come after me.'

'Like a fox before the hounds?'

'More like a rabbit running away from a poacher and his dog.' Raphael chuckled.

'Why is that funny?'

'It's a reference to a previous conversation. You had to be there really.'

'I'm probably glad that I wasn't.' Cat looked anxiously down the corridor. 'How will I know when it's safe to go home?'

'There will be a report in the news about the death of Sir Desmond Swann. The details will all be fabricated, but he will be dead. You can start your life again at that point.'

'Are you going to...?' Cat struggled to frame the question. 'Was that always the purpose of your mission, to assassinate Swann?' She stepped back a half-pace.

'You have to go back in there now,' he said, easing the door open. 'Remember, three minutes from the second you turn the lock.'

Cat nodded slowly. She let him put a hand on her shoulder and guide her inside.

'Good luck,' she said softly as he closed the door.

Raphael listened to the sound of the door locking before setting off down the corridor. It was easy to be silent with the thick carpet beneath his feet.

His first target was still in place, reading the magazine. Raphael walked calmly into view. It was such a natural, unhurried approach, the man's brain didn't recognise the threat until Raphael was within five paces of him. Then he leapt to his feet, throwing the magazine at Raphael's face.

The monk let the missile determine his tactic. As his opponent's eyes instinctively followed the magazine's arc, Raphael took advantage of his momentary distraction. He drove forwards and down, turning his right shoulder inwards as it came into contact with the floor, performing a forward roll that crashed into and through the other man's knees and lower legs.

Raphael regained his feet as his opponent fell. He was already screaming. It was clear that his right knee was dislocated. Raphael made no attempt to quieten him. Instead he ran over to the main doors and opened them wide. The man's agonised screams attracted the attention of the men outside almost immediately. When they saw Raphael in the doorway, two raced towards him, the third reached into his pocket for a two-way radio.

Raphael waited for just a couple of seconds before disappearing back inside the building. For an instant he forgot everything that was happening and let his subconscious inform him.

One minute gone.

Two to go.

Raphael charged out of the door and across the patio. The two men were on the first of the six steps, just where he wanted them. The third man was still holding his radio, having discovered no doubt that no one was answering. He was rushing to catch up.

Raphael saw the shared looks of confusion as the men realised he was attacking rather than fleeing. The two on the steps hesitated briefly. Raphael had gambled that they would. Hunters invariably lost their way when the hunted turned on them without warning. Only the most experienced could manage the sudden shift in adrenalin without it disrupting their movement and emotional state. The two men looking up at him were good, but not that good. They were recovering from their shock more quickly than most, but they had lost a vital second. It was all Raphael needed.

'Run, rabbit, run,' he said, a cold smile creasing his face.

The men reached the fourth step before Raphael was upon them. He had the high ground and had no intention of waiting for them to reach it. Instead he maintained his forward momentum, leaping off the patio, delivering a flying knee attack into the chest of the assailant nearest to him.

The man might as well have been hit by a train.

He was hurled backwards and down, cracking the rear of his skull on the steps as he tumbled to the driveway.

Raphael landed lightly on both feet and sprang onto the bottom step. As the second man turned, Raphael punched up, transferring his weight, firing his fist into the man's pelvis. The bone fractured. The man's hips gave way. His body doubled over, bringing his head down to meet Raphael's rising elbow strike.

Raphael didn't pause to check the results. Instead he sprinted towards the man with the radio. He was clearly struggling with his colleagues' sudden change of fortune. As a result, he came to an abrupt halt and began reaching behind his back for a weapon. In response, Raphael drew the Sica from its sheath as he ran.

The man produced a Glock G19 and began to raise it, widening his stance and taking a two-handed grip. They were already less than twelve feet apart. Raphael knew that, at that distance, the knife was king. Not even the most accomplished shooter could hope to draw, aim and fire accurately before being cut. Raphael feinted as if he was going to veer left, and as the man responded, he straightened his line of attack.

The man realised the severity of his position and tried to angle away from the threat. It was hopeless. Raphael saw the terror in the man's eyes, as he slashed hard and fast with the Sica. It was a disabling cut across the hand, designed to sever ligaments and tendons and break some of the smaller bones. It did just that.

The man screamed as his hand fell open and the gun dropped to the ground. He reached automatically, clamping his good hand around the wound. Raphael spun in place, driving the butt of the knife into the man's temple. It was a knockout blow. The man collapsed.

Two minutes gone.

Raphael cleaned his blade on the man's jacket and turned his attention to the black Range Rover. It was unlocked and the keys were inside, just as he had expected. No one in their right mind would ever attempt to steal a vehicle – or anything else, for that matter – from Sir Desmond Swann. Raphael jumped inside and drove the car to the patio steps. He left it, with the engine running, and made his way back into the mansion.

He was heading for the study, but first he paused in the entrance hall. He needed to be sure Cat was safe before going any further. The man with the dislocated knee was silent and unmoving. Raphael guessed he had fainted due to the pain. He didn't care. All that mattered now was doing what he had set out to do.

Raphael hid behind a large, oak cabinet just as his subconscious spoke again.

Three minutes gone.

And there she was, ashenfaced, running to the open doors, looking straight ahead.

Raphael waited until he heard the Range Rover move away, then he crossed to a window. He watched Cat speed along the drive and turn right onto the road.

'Travel well,' he said gently.

When the Range Rover was out of sight, he raced to the study. The door was open. So was the entrance to the secure room.

33

Swann was standing inside. The Shroud was on show. The billionaire's narrow face seemed slightly more drawn than before.

'It would appear that, despite my warning, Mack underestimated you,' he said. 'Have you killed him?'

Raphael shook his head. 'I haven't killed any of them.'

'Aren't you full of surprises?' Swann took off his glasses and began to clean them with a white handkerchief. 'I did wonder, though, when you chose to let Eddie live.'

'You knew?'

'Guilty as charged.' Swann replaced his glasses. 'In the end, it was just a lucky accident; the sort you create if you're brave enough to take the initiative. Eddie had been getting more and more wayward. Sooner, rather than later, he was going to cause me a significant problem. So I hired one of the many specialists in my little black book to put him out of my misery.

'It seems the specialist must have arrived not long after you left. He told me that he couldn't believe his luck. Neither could I, it served my purposes perfectly to let Mack believe you were the killer.'

'If only he knew what you'd done.'

'But he never will. By the time he recovers from whatever condition you have left him in, this situation will have moved on considerably.' Swann cocked his head to one side. 'You haven't dealt with my entire team, surely?'

'Seven are out of action, including the two who I'm guessing should have been at the rear of the property. Unfortunately for you, they weren't disciplined enough to keep away from Cat. Unfortunately for them, neither was I.'

'So you are presuming you haven't missed any?'

'I know I haven't. Your eyes just gave it away. I'm afraid that means it's all come down to you and me.'

'Not just the two of us.' Swann reached out with his left hand, touching the edge of the ancient cloth. 'It even feels as if something extraordinary has happened to it, even now, after all this time.'

'Your hands have no right to touch anything holy,'

'Owners have the right to touch and hold everything they own.' Swann stroked the Shroud, running his palm over the wound made by the spear thrust. 'Especially when it is this sacred. Don't you understand? This is the ultimate proof that man has been given permission by God to do whatever he chooses. That's what the crucifixion shows: one sacrificial death to earn us all eternal forgiveness no matter what we do, one resurrection to show us the promise of eternal life. How can you, of all people, fail to see this? Man has been given complete freedom! There is no damnation. Only endless opportunity.'

Raphael stared into the hollow face of the image. Still it failed to move him.

'Only men like you, men who worship money and power, can interpret Christ's death in such a way,' he said. 'The crucifixion and resurrection of Jesus is the ultimate example of transformation, not transaction. God wasn't making a deal with humankind. It wasn't a trade-off. It was the greatest of all lessons about the necessity of dying before rebirth can occur.'

Swann sighed dismissively. 'Is that how you justify killing so many?' He asked. 'Do you tell yourself that you have simply enabled their rebirth? If you had been that Roman centurion, would you have thrust the spear just as eagerly into Jesus' side?'

'Who knows?' Raphael stepped towards the billionaire. 'A centurion was taught never to retreat. I do understand that teaching. At worst, I hold my ground for as long as possible. At best, I go forwards and achieve my objective.'

'The Roman army was invincible until it wasn't,' Swann said. 'It was the best until someone better came along. Just because you are stepping forwards, it doesn't mean you are going to win.'

'You have no one here to help you,' Raphael said. 'No one with a pin-head of power to wield on your behalf.'

'But I do have what I consider to be the answer to my prayers.' Swann reached inside his suit jacket and produced a small, black revolver. He pointed it deliberately at the centre of Raphael's chest.

The monk raised both of his hands into a position of surrender.

'You presumed that, because I can afford to pay others to do my work for me, I'm incapable of doing it for myself?' Swann beamed. 'I have used this gun on three occasions, all with the same, fatal outcome. I limit my use because I do appreciate how killing other humans could so easily become addictive. It is transaction and transformation combined, wouldn't you say?'

Raphael kept his gaze fixed over the other man's shoulders. In the background the image on the Shroud blurred as his peripheral vision took over. He felt the earth beneath his feet. He felt the Sica, hanging securely in its sheath, less than six inches away from his raised right palm.

Raphael knew the weapon Swann was holding. It was a

Ruger LCRx .38. It was light and accurate, an excellent choice for a person who didn't use a gun on a daily basis. It implied that Swann really did know what he was talking about.

Raphael was only vaguely aware that his conscious mind wanted him to focus on Swann's trigger finger. It would take less than five pounds of pressure to fire the gun and, given that no man was faster than a bullet, it made sense to direct his attention there. Only Pietro had trained him too well for that to happen. Instead he submitted to his instinct and let his body coil subtly, ready for action.

'If you are praying for a miracle,' Swann said, 'you are going to be let down. There isn't going to be one. It isn't even a miracle that you made it this far, that's simply the result of Mack letting his emotions get the better of him. My friend – the one who told me all about you – will, no doubt, be surprised that I had to kill you myself. Still, God works in mysterious ways, as they say.'

Raphael felt his heart beating, steady and calm despite the threat. The distance between himself and the billionaire seemed to dissolve.

'I will allow you to kneel,' Swann said, 'if you wish to die on your knees, you can kneel before your God.' His finger tightened fractionally on the trigger. 'But do it now monk, if you must.'

Raphael closed his eyes, bowed his head, and began to lower his body. He sensed a surge of triumph engulf Swann. He felt his right hand move of its own accord. He felt the Sica in his grasp for the briefest moment as he thrust himself across the room in a dive for safety.

A gunshot sounded as Swann fired at the place where Raphael had been. Raphael's eyes opened in time to see his knife flying through the air and Swann pivoting to track him. The Sica turned over once mid-flight before the point of the blade hit its target, piercing Swann's chest, burying itself up to the hilt.

The billionaire staggered back, dropping the revolver. His hands reached for the knife, but their strength had already gone. They barely closed around the handle, before he took another faltering step back as if still being driven by the knife.

Raphael regained his footing. Swann glared at him and tried to speak but failed. Coughing up blood, he fell backwards into the Shroud before collapsing onto the floor. Raphael watched the billionaire die, staring up at the image of a resurrected man.

When the body had finally stopped twitching, Raphael withdrew and cleaned the knife. Then he stepped back and looked again at the Shroud. A part of him wanted to prostrate himself and beg forgiveness for what he had done in its presence. Only his heart would not be moved. Even now, the most holy of objects failed to touch him.

Feeling lost and unworthy, Raphael stood next to Swann's body and said a quiet prayer for the soul of the man he had just killed. Then he went back into the study and made a phone call. It was answered almost immediately.

'Yes?'

'I have accomplished my mission,' Raphael said. 'The *SS* is in my possession.'

'Dear God...' His handler's voice was reverential. 'I always knew that, with our Lord's blessing, you would be successful. And what of the previous owner?'

'He has been addressed.'

'With terminal efficiency?'

'As you ordered.'

'This is excellent news.'

'What do you wish me to do now?'

There was a brief silence. Raphael heard his handler's breath as he considered his reply.

'Take the object, with all due care and reverence, away from that place. You must do this immediately. Go back to your home.

It is where you will be most safe. Guard our reward with your life. I will be with you tomorrow to relieve you of your burden.'

The phone line went dead.

The monk cleaned blood from his hands before he touched the holy cloth.

PART III

THE MAN WITH NOTHING...

34

The man known as Raphael Ward arrived back at his home late that night.

The kennels were in darkness. Several dogs barked as he pulled the Volvo into the quadrangle; the rest soon joined in. He parked in front of his house, got out of the car and spent a moment staring up at the dark shadow of the hills.

Then he looked at the stars, further away than he could even imagine. He enjoyed the feeling of being infinitesimally small. The dogs fell silent. He knew that Mia was waiting patiently to greet him.

Raphael opened the car boot and removed a strong, moulded transport case made of black polyethylene. He had found it in Swann's secure room. He had placed the Shroud inside it. Swann, he reflected, had been wrong. The cloth did not feel as if something extraordinary had happened to it, at least not to his hands.

Raphael locked the Volvo, tucked the case under one arm and went inside. The house seemed more barren than he remembered it. He felt a million miles away from the hustle and bustle of London and the wealth of the Berkshire countryside. He put the case down on its wheels and rolled it through the house as he made his way to Mia's run.

She was sitting outside the kitchen door. Her tail wagged furiously when she saw him, but she didn't move. Raphael opened the door, left the case inside, and stepped out to greet her. Her body quivered with excitement, but still she held her place, waiting for permission.

He tested her for a few more seconds and then said, 'Come.'

Mia leapt towards him. He caught her at chest height and accepted her uncontrolled welcome. Finally, he released her and she landed lightly on all fours, spinning in place, desperate to play. Now that he had returned, all was good in Mia's world.

In contrast, he felt as if the beating heart had been ripped out of his. He wondered briefly where Cat was. He guessed the news of Swann's death would become public knowledge in the next couple of days. She would know then that it was safe to return home and that her brother had been truly avenged.

Raphael nodded and gave his attention to Mia. For ten minutes he encouraged her to run and jump, to pull and tug. Then he called an end to the game. Mia followed him inside and lay down on the kitchen floor. The hint of wildness in her eyes told him that she was ready for a hill run.

'Sorry girl,' he said, 'not tonight.'

Mia lowered her head onto her paws and half-closed her eyes. Raphael sat at the kitchen table. The transport case was by his side. He stared at the cold, hard man-made material. Even now he couldn't quite believe what was inside it. He couldn't quite believe it was here, in his home amid the Derbyshire hills.

The line jumped back inside his mind.

Everything has to be somewhere.

Then where was his faith? Where had it gone? Raphael

stood up. Mia raised her head. 'Guard,' he said, pointing at the case.

Mia sat on her haunches.

He walked into the hall and opened the door in the stairwell. He followed the unlit steps down into the basement. The darkness of his meditation room, his place of worship, was indifferent to his presence. He tried to rekindle the connection that had always been there. He tried to open his chest and greet it with his heart. He tried sitting on his meditation cushion and surrendering himself to Mother Earth. He tried praying out loud and praying silently. Nothing worked. The darkness felt like prison walls.

After maybe an hour he returned upstairs. He took a New Revised Standard version of the Bible from the bookshelf in the hall and went back to the kitchen table. Mia had not moved. Raphael looked at her as he opened the book at random, letting the pages reveal what they may.

They fell open at the Gospel of Mark. Chapter one, verses twelve and thirteen. It was Mark's brief introduction to the temptations of Jesus. The words seemed to leap off the page: 'And the Spirit immediately drove him out into the wilderness. He was in the wilderness forty days, tempted by Satan; and he was with the wild beasts...'

They were verses that Father Antonio had returned to repeatedly in his sermons; it was Scripture Raphael had contemplated many times in his monk's cell. Even now he could hear Antonio's voice sharing the most profound wisdom with his dedicated congregation.

'Notice,' he said, 'that our Lord, Jesus, had to be driven out into the wilderness. What does that tell you, my friends? Have you ever been driven – forced – to do something, to face a challenge, you were unwilling to address? Have you ever known what you had to do, but found yourself lacking the motivation and the courage to do it? Of course you have. And our Lord – in human form, sharing the human condition with us – felt the same way.

'Who would ever find it easy to be alone in the darkness for such a long period of time? Especially when surrounded by the wilderness – or the wildness, as we might think of it. It is the wildness that is made up of human doubts and fears, of inadequacy and ego, of desire and the need for power. These are the wild beasts that Mark refers to. These are Satan's weapons.

'Jesus was not driven to confront external forces and dangers. No, he was driven to confront those things we all possess within us: the seeds of our own destruction, the barriers we can so easily build that cut us off from the rest of humanity and blind us to God's presence.'

Raphael remembered sitting in the simple Church, listening to Antonio speak, captivated by the joy in his eyes and the love in his voice. At first, he could not understand why the old man had repeated the same lesson so frequently. Over time, though, and with Pietro's guidance, he had come to appreciate the value and need of repetition.

'We can only draw from the depths we have been to,' Pietro taught. 'If you study and meditate in a joyous and disciplined way, you will find that each time you revisit something, whether that is a holy text, or a place, or even a memory, you will discover something you had not seen before.'

Raphael realised his hand was pressing heavily on the pages of the Bible as his teacher's words reinforced his sense of separation and loss.

He looked again at the transport case. 'Tomorrow I will be

freed of my responsibility to you,' he said. 'Perhaps then I can begin to understand what is happening to me.'

He closed the Bible.

Mia rose to her feet suddenly, her nose exploring the air. She growled, low and deep.

35

Raphael came to his feet, turning off the kitchen light, as the other dogs began to voice their warnings too. He tapped his thigh, sprinted into Mia's compound and opened the gate. She was by his heel, her eyes fixed firmly on him. She was as alert as he had ever seen her.

There were intruders on the premises. He couldn't know where, nor how many. He could, however, guess who was leading them and what their intentions were.

'I should have known a headbutt wouldn't put him out of action for long,' he whispered to his dog. 'Are you ready for this, girl?' Mia barked once and her tail whipped behind her. He touched her left ear fondly. 'It's my fault,' he said. 'I shouldn't have left them alive. I'm sorry for what we now must do.'

Raphael raised his face to the night sky and issued the one-syllable command.

'Kill'.

She was gone in a heartbeat.

He rushed back into the house, grabbed the transport case and took it down into the basement. He retraced his steps. The Sica was now in his hand, the six-inch blade hidden, running along the length of his inner forearm. As he turned right into the hall, a figure dressed all in black launched at him from the shadows of the dining room.

The impact knocked Raphael off his feet. He crashed into the wall, landing on his back with the figure on top of him, straddling his chest and pointing a gun at his face. The monk's hands crossed in a blur. The edge of his right hand struck the man's wrist whilst, simultaneously, his left palm struck the back of the gun hand. The weapon flew from the man's grasp; he cursed, but made no attempt to retrieve it. Instead, he bent his right arm and drove a ferocious elbow strike down towards Raphael's face.

The monk twisted his torso and met the incoming blow with a right elbow strike of his own, using the blade to hack into the man's lower arm. The force of his own movement was enhanced by his assailant's downward momentum. Raphael felt the Sica hit bone and the man grunted in pain. Still, though, he tried to press home his attack, punching down with his left fist towards Raphael's face.

It was a blow designed to break anything it hit, but Raphael was one beat ahead. Having rendered the man's right arm useless, he had already determined what was coming next. He parried the punch with his own right arm whilst slashing the blade forcefully into and across the man's bicep. Blood spurted as the brachial artery severed. The man screamed and tried to stand up.

Raphael took advantage of his movement and drove himself upright, tumbling the man down as he did so. When he had regained his feet, Raphael automatically stamped down hard on both of the man's ankles, fracturing them.

The man passed out and Raphael left him to his fate as blood pumped onto the hall floor.

He ran out into the quadrangle. A Range Rover was parked

near the entrance. The dogs in the kennels were going wild. There was no sign of Mia. Raphael paused, straining to hear what was happening beyond the cacophony of noise. Mack was here somewhere, and he would have at least one other man with him.

So where were they?

Raphael turned slowly through a tight three hundred and sixty degrees. There was no sign of anyone. It occurred to him to run back inside the house, get the keys to the kennels and release all the dogs. Although they couldn't all be relied upon to join in the fray, it would certainly create a level of chaos that would be to his advantage.

Raphael scanned the quadrangle a final time and spun back towards the house. At that moment, he saw another black-clad figure coming out of the darkness. They were twenty feet apart and the man's gun was already raised and aimed. Everything was in his assailant's favour. There was nowhere Raphael could hide, no easily accessible escape route. He heard the man speak into a two-way radio.

'I have him here, dead to rights, in front of house.' Raphael prepared himself for one last, futile charge. The man said, 'Will do,' and lowered his aim from Raphael's chest to his lower stomach.

The monk gripped the Sica tightly and took a deep breath.

The man laughed when he saw the knife. 'You know what they say about bringing a knife to a gunfight,' he said. 'The first shot's going in your guts. The Boss wants you to suffer.' He adjusted his stance fractionally, planting his feet more firmly. 'Then he's going to kill you himself.'

Mia appeared from nowhere. The first Raphael saw was her body leaping through the air, teeth bared. She latched on to the gunman's left arm as her body flew into him. He fired a shot into the air before dropping the gun, staggering under the weight and fury of her attack. Raphael heard her growling as she shook her head furiously, desperate to tear his flesh. The man struggled to regain his balance, punching into her ribcage. Mia released her hold.

She dropped to the floor and sprung immediately for his throat. He twisted to one side. She missed her target, her teeth snapping violently in mid-air. The man pulled a knife from his belt and waved it aggressively towards her face. Mia lowered her body, feinted left then right, and charged in low, aiming for his Achilles. He tried to kick her away. She dodged his boot and risked a bite at his inner thigh. The knife slashed down towards her eyes. She danced away in the nick of time.

Raphael was about to call her off, when he heard an unexpected noise. He spun round to face the house. Mack was in the doorway. Flames were visible in both the lounge and the dining room. They were already licking at the ceilings and spreading into the hall. The house groaned for a second time as the fire took hold.

Mack hesitated, clearly surprised by what was happening in front of him. A split-second later, he was reaching for his gun. Raphael was already halfway towards him, but he knew that he was in danger of being two steps too slow.

Mack moved away from the house, forcing Raphael to slow down and change direction. Mack's Glock came free. He raised easily it and accurately.

Definitely two steps too slow.

Raphael tried to increase his pace. Behind him he could hear Mia growling as her battle raged. He was only vaguely aware of the heat coming from the house.

Mack's eyes glittered with hate. His face was severely bruised and swollen. The pistol was rock-solid in his grasp.

Raphael tried one desperate ploy. 'Better not miss,' he shouted. 'Remember, this one's for your brother!'

Mack snarled a reply and pressed the trigger violently. The bullet whizzed past Raphael's shoulder. By then he had closed the gap. The Sica slashed Mack's right forearm. His hand opened automatically, and the gun dropped to the ground. Seemingly impervious to the pain, Mack leapt away from Raphael's next attack. He used his left hand to produce a heavy, rubber cosh from inside his jacket.

The two men circled each other. 'I'm too good for you,' Mack hissed.

'Maybe,' Raphael replied, 'but not here, not tonight. Tonight, I win for one very simple reason.'

'What's that?' Mack lunged forwards, aiming a strike at Raphael's knife hand.

'You're too emotional.' Raphael pulled back and the blow missed by inches. 'You've got to get past your brother to get to me – and you can't because he's filling your mind.'

Mack screamed in rage and attacked again. This time he threw a stamping kick at Raphael's lead leg, followed by two wild swings at his head.

The monk avoided them all, but as he did so he lowered the Sica briefly, exposing the left side of his face. Mack leapt at the opportunity, swinging a powerful blow at Raphael's temple.

It was precisely what Raphael had wanted. He stepped inside the attack, blocking it with his left forearm, thrusting the blade up into Mack's chest. He felt the point of the Sica hit the resistance of a covert stab-proof vest and realised instantly that he had been tricked.

As Raphael withdrew the blade, Mack struck again. This time the dense rubber cosh thudded heavily into the monk's skull. Raphael staggered and a second blow drove him, helpless, to the ground. It felt as if the Earth was offering itself as his final home.

Mack's roar of triumph merged with the sound of the fire raging through the house. The last thing Raphael saw before his eyes closed was Mia sprinting towards him.

36

Time stopped.
Awareness stopped with it.
Nothingness engulfed him completely.
Death was absolute.

37

He didn't choose to open his eyes and he certainly didn't force himself to do it. His eyes just opened. His other senses followed their lead. Pure white filled his vision. Eventually he realised it was a ceiling. Later, he realised he was in a hospital room. Later still, he became aware of the person sitting next to him. She said nothing until he was able to speak. When he did, his voice was hesitant.

'G— Gemma?'

'Yes.' Somehow he knew there was relief in her voice. That knowing filled him with confidence. 'What happened?'

'Don't you remember?'

'No.' Raphael pressed his head back into his pillows. Bright images filled his mind. He saw a night sky. 'It was hot and painful and...'

Gemma reached out and took his hand. She squeezed it gently. 'You were attacked at the kennels,' she said softly. 'The police think it was a gang that have been targeting isolated country businesses for some time now. You managed to fight them off, until you were hit on the head. The emergency services were there quickly because the gang set fire to your house.'

Gemma paused before she continued.

'The flames were seen and reported. It seems that the fire was enough to make those who could, flee from the scene. The police did find the remains of one man and, incredibly, it seems that Mia killed one other. She was guarding your body when the first police officers, fire engines and ambulance crew arrived. She wouldn't let anyone near you, so they called me. Thank God! The other option under discussion was to shoot her, as it was clear you were in a bad way.

'Once I had Mia under control, you were brought here. The blows you had suffered were significant. You actually died three times before they were able to stabilise you. The truth is no one expected you to live.'

He stared up at the white ceiling. 'What kept me alive?'

'The medical staff told me what they did, but they also said that doesn't explain everything. The man who hit you used an incredibly hard object and he either knew what he was doing or he was lucky, because the blows landed on very vulnerable spots.'

'Perhaps that explains why my head aches so much?'

Her smile came more willingly than his; her smile didn't hurt.

'How long have I been here?' He asked.

'Two days,' Gemma replied.

'And how long have you been here?'

'I divided my time up between you and making sure the dogs are all OK.'

'There was no need – to be here with me, I mean.'

'Of course there was.' Gemma released his hand. 'How is it that you have no family, that the police could find such little information about you?'

'My parents abandoned me when I was young,' he said, repeating the lie he had been taught many years before. 'I grew up in a number of foster homes in Italy. My background made me want to be self-sufficient and live off the grid as much as possible.'

'I can't imagine being without a family,' she said.

'I've made my own,' he said, looking directly at her for the first time since he had regained consciousness.

She smiled and her eyes watered.

'How is Mia?' He asked.

'It's pretty obvious she's missing you, but apart from that she's fine. I moved her in with me for the time being.'

'And the other dogs?'

'They are all temporarily re-homed. We know enough people to call in a few favours. Everyone was willing to help.'

'You said the police found the remains of one man?'

'Yes.'

'So the house...?'

'It was burnt down. I'm sorry. By the time the fire engines arrived, it was too late.'

Raphael tried to force himself upright. His body failed to respond. 'What about the—?'

'What?' Gemma leant forwards.

'The. the contents of my home?'

'Nothing survived I'm afraid. Everything inside the house was destroyed.'

Raphael fell silent.

'I'm really sorry for your loss,' Gemma said.

'It happened before the fire,' he replied, regretting it instantly.

'What do you mean?'

'I mean my – our – business was ruined from the instant the gang targeted us,' he said quickly. 'It's impossible to have credibility as an elite provider of protection dogs when you can't keep yourself safe.'

'The kennels are all intact,' Gemma said. 'We can start working with dogs again just as soon as you are ready. And we never claimed to offer certainty. We just promised to increase peoples' security. You told me that years ago.'

It was true. It was the nearest he had ever come to sharing Pietro's wisdom with her.

'People seek power,' Pietro had said, 'in order to satisfy their ego and because of their desire to create certainty. That is the greatest of all the Devil's illusions. Human beings can no more create certainty than they can keep their bodies alive forever.'

Raphael sank back into his bed. 'Tell me about the man Mia killed,' he said.

'He was at the side of the house,' Gemma said. 'It looked as if he was making his way round the back and Mia met him head on. She must have been so stressed she panicked, because she jumped at him and took out his throat. I explained to the detective in charge that we don't train any of our dogs to attack in that way.'

'I'm glad you said that.' Raphael was suddenly tired. His eyes were heavy. It felt as if the ceiling was pressing down on him. In every sense his mission and his life had been a failure. The holy Shroud of Turin had been burnt asunder because of his incompetence. Mack, the man responsible, had escaped. Beyond that, he had let Gemma down.

He fell asleep hoping he would never wake up again.

38

He did.

It was the next day and he felt stronger than the time before. As his health returned, he waited for the police to visit and question him. Instead, his phone rang.

He recognised his handler's voice instantly. 'You lost everything?'

'Yes.'

'Even the object you had retrieved?'

'Yes.'

'Your failure is a consequence of your bad decision making.'

'I know.'

'And your failure is beyond compare. You have let down Mother Church in ways I could never have imagined. You have made me look stupid in the eyes of those around me.'

'I can only tell you how deep my regret is.'

'I pray that your regret springs from a well that will never run dry.'

There was a moment of silence between them.

'The local police have been directed in this matter by someone of much greater seniority than they,' his handler continued. 'Consequently, they will not be searching for those who attacked you. They will not be questioning you. They will not be treating your dog as a dangerous animal. They believe there is an issue of national security involved; one that is of such significance all else must simply fade away.'

'Thank you.'

'You do not need to thank me. This wasn't done for your protection, I assure you.'

'Of course,' Raphael lay back in his bed. He noticed a dark spot on the ceiling that he hadn't seen before.

'In this world of constant media and noise, it is difficult enough for our work to remain in the shadows,' his handler said. 'It is almost impossible to do so when you light up the night with fire.'

'Mack wanted to destroy everything,' Raphael said. 'He believed that I killed his brother.'

'Swann took advantage of your presence to create a falsehood.'

'Yes.'

'You made it easy for him to do so.'

'Yes.'

'There will be a meeting in a few days' time to discuss your future with us,' his handler said. 'The older leaders amongst us still believe in forgiveness, they are minded by our Lord's teaching, they are loath to cast stones. If they hold sway, you will be given opportunities to redeem yourself. You need to be clear, however, that I will be arguing against such a notion and, regardless, I will never work with you directly again.'

Raphael was not surprised. The cold, hard anger in the other man's voice had been evident throughout.

'You will be informed of the outcome in due course,' the voice said. 'Inevitably, the incident at your home has been deemed newsworthy and reports have appeared in the public domain. Sadly, even we cannot control everything.'

'I understand.'

'I doubt it.' His handler sniffed. 'However, if you are approached by any journalists please do ensure you say nothing and do present yourself as a confused and scared victim. Can you manage that?'

'Yes.'

'I truly hope so. We need this to die swiftly.'

Raphael thought of the many men he had killed.

'And with that,' his handler said, 'I will say goodbye.'

'There is one thing before you go,' Raphael said quickly.

'Which is?'

'Swann's shoes.'

'What?'

'The soles of his shoes were unmarked and spotless. Just like yours.'

The call ended abruptly.

Raphael let the phone rest in his hand as he replayed the conversation in his mind. In all likelihood his time working for the Mystiko Kataskopos was over. His name would be erased from their annals. If he were ever spoken of again, it would be as their greatest disgrace. His future would still be built on a history that never happened and a name that wasn't his, only now it would all be for nothing. Raphael sat up and swung his legs over the side of the bed. He was momentarily dizzy, blood pounding in his brain. When it subsided, the statement hit him as hard as Mack's cosh.

Swann took advantage of your presence to create a falsehood.

How could his handler have possibly known that? Swann had shared it simply as a way of further emphasising his power. Raphael had subsequently told no one. Mack still blamed him for Eddie's death. So how could his handler know it was a falsehood?

There was only one answer. Even now Raphael didn't want to believe it, but he was forced to.

His handler had been Swann's informant. He was the betrayer of the MK.

Raphael looked at his phone and considered his options.

There were none.

Not now, at least. He had no way of contacting any of the elders; he didn't even know their identities. The only person he could call was his handler, and what good would that do, other than alert him to the fact that Raphael had worked it out?

No, right now all he could do was wait to hear the results of the meeting about his future with the MK. If, as he suspected, they closed their doors to him, then he was powerless in the matter. If, for some miraculous reason, they let him stay, he would regain their confidence and seek to expose his handler.

Raphael pushed himself off the bed. The room tried to spin around him, but he refused to give it permission. If he possibly could, he was going to forget the Mystiko Kataskopos for a while and focus on rebuilding a business that he loved.

Before that, he had to show his gratitude and love to Gemma.

39

They met in the open, grassed training field to the side of the quadrangle and kennels. She had brought Mia with her. The dog leapt to greet him. He caught her, as she knew he would. Gemma stood back and let the pair have their moment.

When it was over and Mia was back on the ground, Gemma said, 'I thought you were supposed to stay in hospital for at least two more days?'

'I'm sure there's someone who needs that bed more than I do,' he replied.

'Do you know how pale you look?'

'I'm trying to avoid mirrors.'

'I think that's probably a wise move.'

They began to walk slowly across the field. Mia ran around them, keeping a close eye on Raphael.

'We've trained some beautiful dogs here,' Gemma said. 'We'll train many more yet. That is, if you're willing to give me a bit more time before you move on to set up your own place.'

Her face lit up. 'You're definitely going to continue here?'

'Of course. I've already rented an apartment in the village, whilst the house is being rebuilt. Other than that, we can let people know it's business as usual, and remind them that we are the best there is.'

'That sounds exciting!'

'There will come a time, though, when you have to fly the nest. To be honest, you're ready now. I'm just being selfish by asking you to stay a while longer.'

'I'm just being selfish when I say that I'd love to!'

'Good,' Raphael stopped walking.

'There is something else,' he said. 'It's an important business decision that I've made, and I need to share it with you. I'm afraid it's one that isn't open to discussion. I've thought it through, and my mind is made up.'

Gemma looked at him quizzically. 'What is it?'

Raphael reached inside his tracksuit top and removed some papers. He waved them in front of her face. 'It's all to do with these,' he said. 'It's a matter that is going to affect you significantly.'

'What are they?' Gemma tried to take the papers from his hand, but he pulled them away.

'I need you to trust me on this,' he said.

'Tell me what it is!' Gemma reached again. This time she got hold of the papers, but he refused to let them go. 'C'mon!' She said, 'Let me see!'

Raphael tightened his grip. 'It's Falco,' he said. 'These are his papers. I've decided that he'll never make it as an elite protection dog, so I'm giving him to you. It's my way of saying thank you.'

Gemma squealed with delight and kissed him on the cheek. Mia ran to join them, barking as she darted around their legs.

'I can't believe you're doing this!' Gemma said.

'I'm not doing it, it's done.' Raphael let go of the papers. 'He's all yours. I'm sure he'll be as happy as you are.'

She kissed him a second time. 'Talking of giving things, there is something that I have for you,' she said. 'It was posted to the kennels whilst you were unconscious in hospital. It was forwarded to me and I forgot about it, what with everything going on.'

She handed him a sealed envelope.

He opened it slowly. It contained two newspaper clippings, one about the untimely and unexpected death by heart attack of Sir Desmond Swann, and the other about the attack and fire at the kennels. It also contained a Get Well card. It had a picture of a cat on the front. Inside were written two simple words.

Thank you

Raphael smiled and slipped it inside his jacket, next to his heart.

'Are you going to tell me?' Gemma asked.

'It's from a well-wisher.' He looked up at the hills.

'You're not seriously going for a run up there, are you?'

Gemma took hold of his arm. 'You should be looking after yourself, not stressing your system further.'

'A man can't put a tracksuit on without doing some exercise,' he said.

'My dad does.'

'I promise never to tell him how to run his pub if, in return, he never tells me how to manage my exercise routine.'

'I think you'll both find that easy.' Gemma released her grip. 'You won't push too hard, will you?'

'I don't think I could if I wanted to.' Raphael tapped his thigh with the palm of his left hand. Mia came to heel instantly. 'This is as much for her benefit as it is mine,' he said. 'We both need the hills and the fresh air.'

'Then please make sure you look after each other.

And...'

'And, what?'

'Just send me a text once you're back safely.'

40

Raphael had done his best to feign exasperation, but he had failed miserably. Gemma had simply laughed at him, refusing to let him go until he promised to message her.

That had been forty-five minutes ago. Now he and his dog were nearing the summit. Raphael's heart was pounding, and his skin was drenched in sweat. It felt like the hardest run of his life, but it also felt like the best one. When they reached the top, he placed his phone on the usual rock and gave himself time to slow his breathing. Then he stood, facing the horizon as he always did, and closed his eyes. He could tell that Mia had positioned herself nearby. He guessed she was watching him closely. Raphael tried to shift his awareness into the back of his brain and his body. It should have been the easiest thing in the world, but the longer he stood there, the more the Earth felt as if it was spinning beneath his feet. The sensation grew until he was forced to open his eyes and seek balance. His hands reached out, grasping at thin air.

Mia darted to his side, barking anxiously.

Raphael shook his head and the situation worsened. He staggered as the planet turned and twisted like a crazy fairground ride. He was sure the sky was rushing down to touch the hilltop. His chest felt as if it was going to explode. His vision blurred. Suddenly, the horizon came charging towards him like a tidal wave and knocked him off his feet.

Darkness descended. His senses were lost within it.

This time Death – if that is what grasped him – was not absolute. The nothingness gave way to the familiar vision of the deserted, twisting country road, lined with trees and bushes. It beckoned him and he accepted its invitation, stepping out of himself and onto it.

Here, he felt light and free. He began to run, increasing his pace without effort. He heard the birds singing more clearly than he ever had. He felt the breeze on his face, soothing and energizing. He knew that it came from every place on Earth – and beyond.

He ran because the road pulled him, and he trusted its direction. He ran because his heart told him to. He ran because he felt both driven and drawn.

He followed the road without once imagining where it might lead. He knew, somehow, that he had left his thoughts behind. They were inside his body, laying on the summit with his dog holding guard.

Finally, the road turned one final bend and he reached his destination. He stopped running and stared at what was in front of him.

A voice that seemed as familiar as the sun, said, 'Welcome home.'

41

The next morning Raphael Ward asked Gemma to look after Mia one more time and drove away without telling her where he was going.

The vision of the day before seemed to have lasted only a few minutes, but had kept him pinned to the hilltop for hours. When he finally opened his eyes, the night was already making its move over the horizon. By the time he had reached his rented apartment, it was already dark. When he finally remembered to look at his phone, he had a scared and angry message from Gemma demanding to know how he was. His reply had been both apologetic and reassuring.

After that he fed and watered Mia but wanted nothing for himself. He tried to sleep, but his eyes refused to close. He tried to think, but his mind had disappeared. He sat, unmoving, for hours and then watched the sun rise.

When Gemma asked how long he would be away for, he told her he didn't know. It was the truth. He didn't know how long his journey would take, because he didn't know where his destination was. Something, however, was drawing him to Wales, to the hills and mountains of Snowdonia.

He took the M56, kept to the speed limit, and arrived there in less than three hours. Then he followed one country road after another, trying to let his intuition guide him. For a while he kept getting in his own way, convincing himself that he could sense the route when, in reality, he knew he was trying to make something happen. Finally, he accepted the impossibility of the task and drove through the countryside with a smile on his face. The land was both beautiful and commanding, a place of legend and myth, and mystical powers. Raphael meandered through it, entranced by its majesty. Such was the hold it exerted over him he lost all sense of direction and time.

Suddenly, the road turned through a series of tight corners and, at once, he recognised it. This was the road in his vision, the place that had been appearing to him repeatedly in recent months.

Raphael increased his speed; desperate to discover if it led to the place he had seen. The road narrowed, the twists and turns becoming more frequent, forcing him to slow down. He had no choice but to accept its restrictions. He found it easy to think of it as a lesson. He found the lesson difficult to manage. His desire and expectation were making his heart race. He counted the beats, using it as a method of distraction.

Sixty-eight beats per minute.

He couldn't remember a time when it had ever been anywhere near that high. He forced himself to concentrate on his driving. In places, the hedgerows reached out and scratched the edges of the car. In others, the branches of the trees lining either side of the road met each other, forming a canopy above. Eventually, when it seemed that he had been on the road forever, he reached the final bend.

The stone-built cottage it led to was just as it had been in his vision. Only now a grey-haired old man was standing outside.

He raised a lined, powerful hand in greeting as a lean, mongrel dog padded into view.

Raphael parked the car and got out.

'We've been expecting you,' the old man said, gesturing to the dog and a black-haired cat that was curled up by the front door. 'Why don't you come in, you've had an awfully long journey.'

42

Raphael followed the old man into a simple kitchen. The dog and the cat stayed outside. The old man poured Raphael a glass of water. 'Sip this as I talk,' he said. 'You're going to need it. And, please, take a seat.'

Raphael lowered himself into one of the two wooden chairs by the table. 'I really don't understand what's happening,' he said. 'I don't know why I'm here.'

'Everyone travels for the same reasons,' the old man said. 'It's either to hear something, or to see something. In your case, it's both.' He sat in the other chair. 'I think it's best if you hear what I have to say, before you see what I have to show you. Is that OK with you?'

Raphael nodded.

'Good.' The old man pointed at the glass with a stubby finger. 'Remember to sip the water. It's good for you.'

Raphael took a sip.

'Let's start at the beginning,' the old man said. 'I mean at the beginning of our problem – the world's problem – the very greatest problem of all time, the problem we have failed to acknowledge or address throughout history.

'It is simply this: our planet has always been controlled and defined by men. It is men who have created the structures and systems that make societies work. It is men who determine both cultural and geographical boundaries. It is men who have established a world in their own image. It is men who continue to deny the leading part they have played, and continue to play, in the destruction of our environment and the spiritual deficit in our lives.

'Even our Church was formed by men, who turned it quickly into a political power. They use the great organisation of the Church to define, control and contain the faithful. This is the opposite of what our Lord Jesus and, indeed, all of the other great mystics taught.

'The mystics challenged and dared people to turn inward and discover their true heart, their original heart. They taught ways of transformation, not containment. They taught that a person's greatest battle lay within themselves, not with others.

'In my humble opinion, Jesus was a true leader because he offered himself as a servant and as a role model. He was a great teacher because, through his parables and his actions, he invited introspection and self-discovery. He was a most significant guide, because he pointed the way and dared us to have the courage to follow, to have the courage to let go of the illusions created by men, the courage to find the hidden truth within the human condition.'

The old man gestured again at Raphael's glass. The monk forced himself to have another sip.

'And that hidden truth is one of harmony,' the old man went on. 'The mystics knew – Jesus knew – that harmony is always present, even in the most turbulent of times. No matter what discord men manufacture, no matter how violent and disconnected the world seems, harmony remains. It runs untouched below the surface, like a current that cannot be noticed from the shoreline. Men think that harmony can be built, when in fact it is there already, waiting to be felt, offering to draw us back to our original selves.

'We are living now in the most dangerous of times. The grip of arrogant, self-righteous men is tightening. The lies they have told, that have been told throughout history, are being reinforced. It is with a heavy heart, I must tell you that even our Church plays its part in this.'

Raphael couldn't help but think of his handler.

'It is one of the Church's greatest lies that I am about to reveal to you,' the old man said. 'It relates to your most recent search.'

Raphael pushed his glass to one side. 'How can you possibly know about that?' He asked.

'It is possible to travel the world without leaving your own home.' The old man slid the glass back towards Raphael. 'That is something you will learn to appreciate in the coming years. You are still a young man, still relatively inexperienced in the contemplative path. Over time, you will come to realise it is a path that has no boundaries and no limits.'

Raphael took a swallow of water.

'You were sent to retrieve what you were told was the original Shroud of Turin,' the old man continued. 'You believe you failed to protect it and that it has been destroyed. You are wrong on both counts.

'The object you retrieved was not the genuine Shroud. Your handler knew that. The most senior clerics in the Church also knew that. Their most shameful secret is not that the Nazis stole the Shroud during the Second World War. It is something far worse. I know, because I am the protector of the true Shroud.'

'What?' Raphael jumped to his feet. 'How can that possibly be?'

'The Church owned the true Shroud only briefly, early on its history. Even then it was their most secret and prized possession. A few hundred years after the death of Jesus, when it became clear that his teachings were being changed to suit the creation of a formal, well-organised and political religion, this Shroud was stolen.

'A small group from those known as the Desert Fathers and Mothers took it. They were Christian mystics, hermits and monks, who moved away, mainly into the Scetes desert of Egypt, to dedicate themselves to following Jesus' real example.

'Despite its best efforts, the Church has never reclaimed this Shroud. Since its time in the desert, it has been kept, hidden and protected, in the most humble of places.'

'But why would you want to keep it from the Church?' Raphael paced the tiny room.

'Because, I am ashamed to say, it would not be safe in the Church's hands. It reveals their greatest lie and challenges their very foundation.'

'How can that be?'

The old man rose slowly. 'Follow me,' he said. 'I will show you.'

He led the way into the room at the rear of the cottage. Another, even larger, table dominated the space. A simple, woollen blanket lay over it. 'For obvious reasons, I normally keep the Shroud out of sight,' the old man said, 'but in anticipation of your arrival I laid it out. Look.' He removed the blanket.

Raphael stared at the linen cloth that lay before him. The image that looked back was clear and unmistakable. The face radiated love. It penetrated his soul. Raphael fell to his knees in supplication, with tears streaming down his face.

The image was that of a woman.

43

The old man waited until Raphael was able, once again, to listen.

'There never was a shroud with the image of Jesus on it,' he said. 'The truth of the resurrection was revealed here, on the burial shroud of his mother, Mary. It is her image that was miraculously transferred when she ascended into heaven. She, the mother of Jesus, was the holiest of all. She submitted herself completely to the will of the Lord. She gave up her life and all her expectations to serve. She is the shining example from every angle.

'Jesus knew this throughout his life. He gave us so many clues during his Ministry. Just think of the many occasions he spent with women, emphasising their importance, ignoring the social norms of the time.

'A male-dominated Church could never reveal to the world that their most holy relic was of a woman, that it was the Mary Shroud. Rather, they made use of fakes, showing the body of a man, using them to reinforce their lie. Even the revelations of the carbon dating in 1988 were preferable to, and certainly far easier to manage than, this.'

'But the Church venerates Mary,' Raphael said.

'In her role as the vessel through which God became man, not as she should be – as the most holy of holies.'

Raphael nodded slowly. 'Why have the MK been tasked with searching for fakes?'

'Primarily to ensure the lie was maintained. There was also the feint possibility that one of you might come across this, the real Shroud. Of course, if you had...'

'We would have been silenced,' Raphael finished the sentence for him.

'Yes, with terminal efficiency.'

Raphael took his eyes away from the cloth for the first time since he had seen it. 'Who are you?' He asked.

'No one special.' The old man smiled softly. 'For reasons I don't yet understand, and perhaps never will, my heart told me to share this with you. So I have. The question now is, what are you going to do with your knowledge?'

Raphael looked again at the Mary Shroud, at the gentle smile playing on the face, even at the time of death. 'I'm going to try and find my way home,' he said. 'And when I do, I'm going to train some dogs.'

'I wish you peace.'

The two men walked outside without saying another word. The dog and the cat hadn't moved. Raphael shook the old man's hand; his grip was still strong.

'God bless.'

Raphael got into the car and drove slowly back along the narrow road. His tears flowed unhindered.

44

The bald, overweight man returned to his office just as his mobile phone rang. He arched an eyebrow when he saw the number.

'This is an unexpected breach of protocol,' he said.

'I'm a former member of the Mystiko Kataskopos,' the man known as Raphael Ward replied. 'That means I'm not subject to your rules and regulations.'

The bald man frowned. 'A former member, you say? The meeting to decide your future hasn't yet taken place.'

'It doesn't need to, that's why I'm calling you. I have made my own decision about my future. You can regard this as my resignation.'

'You think it is within your power to resign your position?'

'Given that I've just done it, I think it must be. Just as it was within my power to contact you.' Raphael moved his mouth closer to the phone. 'I'm not going to kill anymore. And I want to be left alone. Is that clear?'

The line went dead before the bald man could answer. His face creased in anger. He took a moment to calm himself and then made another call. It was answered swiftly.

'We have an unexpected problem with an ex-operative,' he said. 'It needs to be addressed urgently. It requires terminal efficiency.'

With the instruction given, the bald man crossed to the large, double-glazed window and looked out at the familiar view of St Peter's Square, Rome.

'Thank God for the faithful,' he said.

ACKNOWLEDGMENTS

My sincere thanks to all at the West Midlands Police Dogs Training Centre for sharing their time and expertise.

In particular, many thanks to the inimitable Dave Raymond for agreeing to introduce to me to the very specialised world of police dog training, and for being my guide.

Thanks also to Chris Abbott, Tony Brown and Dave Hibbert.

A special thank you also goes to CNC Police Dog Instructor John Kelly and, of course, the marvellous Marcie.

And a big thank you goes, of course, to Betsy and the wonderful team at Bloodhound Books!

A NOTE FROM THE PUBLISHER

Thank you for reading this book. If you enjoyed it please do consider leaving a review on Amazon to help others find it too.

We hate typos. All of our books have been rigorously edited and proofread, but sometimes mistakes do slip through. If you have spotted a typo, please do let us know and we can get it amended within hours.

info@bloodhoundbooks.com

ABOUT THE AUTHOR

Chris Parker's first book, *Chaney's Choice,* was published in 1986. Since then, he has had a further 17 books published. These include an acclaimed thriller series – the Marcus Kline trilogy, including *Influence*, *Belief* and *Faith* – two critically acclaimed poetry volumes, the *City Fox & others in our community* and *debris*, and the Amazon no1 bestseller, *Living In The Moment, The Wisdom of Epiah Khan.*

Chris is an experienced educator, university lecturer and management trainer. He has been practising martial arts and meditation since the 1970s.

Printed in Great Britain
by Amazon